AMANDA SIMONS

*To my brother, who I wish I could show all my work to.
To my dad, who was a big cheerleader for his kids
(to everyone, really).
To my best friend, Ron, who was a fucking amazing artist
(amazing everything). This would have been a fun
collaboration for us.*

And to those who daydream about revenge...

DON'T.

1

▶❙❙

"Beware. The legend is real. Look out for your children or the duendes will look out for them for you. They want to be their friend. They want to pull pranks on them. They want to play. And they want the kids for themselves.

"Don't believe me? Look up a '99 missing child's case. Nevaeh. Merizo, Guam. You'll know the one when you see it. I swore to myself that I would take this story to my grave, but my best fri—sorry—*ex*-best friend, I learned... killed herself. For fifteen years we hadn't spoken after it happened. We were barely ten when I got her wrapped up in my... mess.

"She killed herself and it's all my fault. She wrote to me before she did it. Not email, not text message, not Facebook, and not even a phone call. Nothing that would have let me get to her sooner. Or get help to her sooner. The first thing the letter said was that she never stopped hating me. She explained that she was never able to forgive herself. She was never able to talk about what she had seen that night with anyone, not because I made her swear to God that she would never tell a soul, but because of how ashamed and scared and guilt-ridden she was. She claimed that she became mentally ill with this sickening and dark secret eating her from the inside out. The desperate screams followed her throughout her life. She'd heard it from cheering audiences at baseball games. She'd heard it from children playing at the beach. She'd heard it in horror films, which she'd learned early on was a genre of film she physically couldn't get herself to sit through. She'd heard it in the squawking of birds, screaming tea kettles, even bursts of laughter from people in crowds. Basically, the screaming was just about everywhere, in everything, from everyone all the time.

"When she walked in on what was going on she was appalled to have watched *me*—her best friend, someone she trusted—just watching that... that... *horror show*, and doing nothing about it. But that wasn't even the worst part. The worst part was when Nevaeh had locked eyes with Isa as she reached out for help, right before getting dragged away, never to be seen again. That was the moment that ruined her.

"This memory haunted her every day of her life and she couldn't handle it anymore. I deserved all the hate she had for me. I never blamed her for not wanting anything to do with me. I always wished her well, but especially during my own difficult moments of remembering, because this was eating me alive, too. I would always think 'however bad it was for me, it was twice as bad for her.' Because it was *my* idea. And I involved her in it. Anyway, I'm not trying to throw a pity party for myself. I just finally need to get it out. Not just for me, but for my fri—for Isa. It's too late, and I know that, but I want to absolve her from any fault in the world of the living and hopefully the afterlife as well.

"Isa was a sweet and pleasant person to have been around in elementary school, which is all I can speak to. She knew nothing but kindness until then. This was all on me. Well, me and my duende friend.

Ex duende friend."

"Wow. Woo! What a way to start a podcast, huh guys? That's some shit right there. Now, what's a... a duende, for those of us who aren't from... I'm sorry, what is it? Guata—"

If I had a nickel for every time someone would confuse Guatemala with— "It's Guam."

"Right. Guam." Nathan, the host, is looking at images of the island online. "Oh, wow. Beautiful island. And, uh, is Guam its own country or...?"

If I had a nickel... "Guam is a U.S. territory. And the duendes are a part of CHamoru legends. You hear all kinds of stories about people's children talking to these little gnome-like creatures."

"That's right, folks. Guam has some pretty wild and spooky stories. And today's guest, Maiana Champaco, well, you–you've already revealed quite a lot that's come out of your experience. But in our email exchange, I thought you said this happened when you were little?"

"Correct."

"Alright. Let's rewind a bit. Please, take it from the top."

2

—·—

Maiana/Taya' Respetu

Every morning, every stupid morning, in class we pledge to our island's flag that we will protect and defend and elevate our land, people, and culture. I'm nine. Can you just teach me how to defend myself from my peers? Can you first show me how to get through elementary *and then* I'll defend whatever you need me to? How can I sing Fanohge CHamoru when Nevaeh and Junie are over there doing the Double-Loser and Whatever signs at me? How am I supposed to proclaim the Inifresi in perfect CHamoru enunciation when Tweedledee and Tweedledumb are mouthing *What are you looking at?* at me when I was clearly looking at them hand-signing insults at me in the first freaking place? How am I supposed to co-exist and *"para bai hu protehi"* anything with people who love to start trouble? Tell me. How?

Whatever. I'm over school. I'm over all of these dumb kids. These dumb teachers who won't make them stop. Dumb parents who can't, don't, or won't see that I'm not "acting like a brat" just to act like a brat. Nobody can see or wants to see or tries to see that this is already changing me, and hell, even my underdeveloped brain can see that this spaghetti and meatball set of friends enjoys the thrill of mentally torturing me. Why me? Because I'm the weakest link. My underdeveloped brain can understand the math of

$$1 \text{ weakling} + 2 \text{ little shits} = \text{TROUBLE}$$

Gee, Maiana, can you show your work for that problem? Sure! You see, you have

$$1 \text{ weakling} - \text{mental strength} = 0 \text{ power}$$
$$2 \text{ little shits} + \text{overbearing narcissistic traits} = \text{whatever they want}$$

So, then you get this new equation where

$$0 \text{ power} + \text{whatever the fuck they want} = \text{WHATEVER THE}$$
$$\text{FUCK THEY WANT}$$

Sorry. Excuse my CHamoru. I'm a bitter nine year old. Adversity really forces a child to grow up. While SpongeBob and Patrick are goofing off and terrorizing others I'm just trying to fill my lock-and-key diary with my writing. You see, I already know what I want to be when I grow up. I want to be a writer. While I'm already preparing for my future, all they want is to be popular. While they're thinking of popularity, I'm leagues ahead thinking of *fame*. Not for money, no. I just want some motherfucking respect. And no, do not excuse my CHamoru this time because I don't just mean "respect". I do mean MOTHERFUCKING RESPECT. I get taya' respetu and yet I always have to give it. Always have to be polite. Always have to be courteous. Always have to say sorry if something or someone is making me shy or uncomfortable. Why can't anyone be sorry to me? What about me? Just imagine...

I'm sorry, Maiana, that I didn't stop the bullying when it was my duty as your teacher, your supervisor, as the authority over the class, as the adult in the room, as the caretaker in the absence of all the parents.

We're sorry, Maiana, that we didn't teach you how to properly prevent or ignore or diffuse bullying as your parents. We're sorry we didn't create a safe space for you to tell us about your day so that you had to take it out on us and then get grounded for your attitude without question. We're also sorry that we see the signs that something is wrong but that we're not asking about it and instead only recognizing that it's affecting us.

We're sorry, Maiana, that we tease you for being so quiet and not understanding that you're so quiet because we tease you. We're sorry that we make fun of you for paying attention to the teacher and not getting in trouble with us. We don't pay attention because we know we're fucking morons so we talk during class so that we have a reason as to why we're not understanding the lessons. We're sorry that we're just jealous losers.

The lunch bell rings and it takes me out of my unrealistic dreams of apologies. As I am walking out of the door, Nevaeh, the tall one of my terrorists, the leader, tries to fit through the door frame at the same time I go through. We bump shoulders and then she shoves me into my side of the doorframe to get through first.

"Sorry," I say stupidly, like the cowardly people-pleaser I am. I mean, I didn't want to say it, trust me, but it comes out of me like Helga Pataki's accidental admission of love for Arnold. Junie laughs because she laughs at everything that Nevaeh does, as long as the bullying isn't directed at her.

Isa gives me a hug when I get in line for a lunch tray. We've been friends since kindergarten. I remember sitting with her as we waited for our rides. She had five long sticks of beef jerky—those things were a hot commodity back in the day—and she gave me one. Without having to ask. I accepted because I didn't have money to buy my own. I felt bad that I was too shy to thank her, so the next day I gave her a random book that I hadn't read yet. To say I was shy was an understatement and if not for her I'd probably have been a loner throughout elementary.

"Si yu'us ma'åse, Ms. Mary." The lunch lady appreciates it when I call her by her name, and she always gives me an extra scoop on spaghetti days. Isa and I exit the line and make our way to our usual table. The moment we sit, Isa does her silly hungry dance. She waits for me to do a hungry dance with her but I don't.

"It's spaghetti day, your favorite food, and you're not dancing. What's the matter?" She drops her fork onto her tray and leans back with crossed arms. "It's them again, isn't it?"

I don't say anything because it's embarrassing.

She begins to stuff her face but speaks through her full mouth, "You know, I will never forgive her for stealing my Dunkaroos last year. Didn't even try to hide it. Didn't at least zip my bag closed! Not that she'd ever say sorry or anything." She downs her chocolate milk.

"They were calling me a loser. And then Nevaeh shoved me as we were going out the door." I put my face in my hands, cringing at what I could have done but didn't. "Ughhh. God, why am I like this," I ask, though it comes out muffled.

I hear Isa move to the seat beside me. "Hey," she says, putting my hands down, "how about... how about acting like this is one of your stories? Pretend you're on an adventure. This is just one obstacle. You'll get through it! This is your story and you're the main character. And the main character always lives to tell the tale."

I look at her through my fingers.

"You'll survive. Eat up."

I finish the first ice-cream scoop portion of my favorite lunch food before I continue. "I hate them. I freaking hate them."

"Forget them. Want to come over today? We can play Barbies. I got a whole house of furniture for them. Everything for the kitchen, everything for the living room, everything for the bedroom. Even a bathroom! Like, a toilet that opens and closes and everything. And the fridge is stocked with food. They're so tiny and cute and adorable!"

Ugh. I really don't want to. "I'd love to but I'm still grounded for not doing my chore list. So, I think I'll just do that and do some writing."

"You know, you have the rest of your life to become a famous writer. Barbies!"

"Grounded!"

We laugh at her pathetic and desperate attempt at convincing me.

"Fine. Whatcha gonna write?"

"I don't know. I might sneak out to my spot and feel it out, you know?"

"No, I don't know. But anyway, forget the Tweedles."

"I'm trying. It's just... when will they grow up?"

Isa rolls her eyes. "Ugh, tell me about it. *Kids*. Am I right? Anyway," she wipes her spaghetti-stained mouth on her shirt, leaving a saucy mouth print on it, and retrieves a book from her bag. She slides it across the table to me, "I just finished this over the weekend. It's good. Like, *really* good. My mom said I can let you borrow it, but she said regular-borrow, not CHamoru-borrow."

"Jeez, I'll return it. Don't worry."

"I mean, I know, it's just that she let my auntie borrow our bush cutter and basically sakke'd it and now she has trust issues. I'm sure she was only kidding."

"Mhm." I inspect the book and flip through the pages. "The Giving Tree? It's pretty short." I shrug my shoulders and retrieve my own book for our book-borrowing trades.

"Holy moly, Maiana! That thing is huge!"

My contribution was a 1987 beautiful leather bound Children's Classic edition of Frances Hodgeson Burnett's The Secret Garden, incredibly illustrated in color by Troy Howell. As soon as you open the hardback front cover there is a This Book Belongs To page with my name written on the line, *Maiana Joann Chaco Champaco, 10/8/96, From Mommy*. I can't exactly say if I love the book or not, but I have a fond memory of it. One night, shortly after receiving the book I guess, I don't really remember that moment, but I remember that our power was out. That was probably because Mom and Dad were late paying the power bill—I'm not certain, but they were always worried about the power going off. In the silent darkness she had made a floor bed for me in the living room and read to me this book aloud by candlelight as she stroked my hair. And it was as if I blinked and suddenly, I'm in charge of dishes, defrosting meat for dinner, sweeping, and laundry—and if I don't keep up, I'm grounded.

Isa likes the way the book feels in her hands. She flips through it and admires the pictures. "It feels like a spell book or something. This is actually really nice. Fine. I'll read it because it looks cool."

I smile because I'm happy to lend her something she is impressed by. I'm the one who is normally impressed with all she has. She shares the best snacks, she gives me Bongo shirts that she can't fit anymore, she lets me wear her Hello Kitty watches from morning until the end of the school day. Aside from her Barbie obsession, my friend is super awesome.

The rest of the school day goes about as usual, but it feels like forever. Is this what life is? Just school, school, school forever and always? The same old things? All the time? Everyday? This is no way to live.

The bus ride home is always pretty lonely. Isa gets picked up by her grandma and I normally sit by myself. Well, I don't always sit by myself because other kids need the second seat, but I might as well just be alone on the whole bus. I don't talk to anyone and no one talks to me. Which is fine by me.

When the bus finally drops me off on Quinene Road, I still have a steep road to walk up. It's so steep that the bus driver hates driving up it, so she tells me to just walk the rest of the way, but I don't mind. There's a bunch of trees on both sides of the road but I'm only afraid of what may be lingering unexposed when it's dark.

A couple hours after getting home my parents tell me over the phone that they are going to be home a bit later. That usually means that they are going to hang out with some people after work, but they always bring me back a to-go plate of food so I don't mind all that much.

I cook myself an ichiban, the typical after school food of the island, right when I get home and put on Nickelodeon. Rugrats is playing on channel 27. When I finish my food, I decide it's time to take a walk to my writing spot. I'm not supposed to go alone, but I'll be careful. I always am.

My spot is not on the sandy beach, which is a farther walk, but on the rocky inlet on the way. I sit on the grass underneath a palm tree and watch as the light glistens on the water that empties into an endless ocean. The sound of the crashing waves is the sound of home. It's my comfort. It is my peace. The light sparkles and refracts off the water and I like to imagine they are thousands of little fairies dancing. To share a world with magical creatures just beyond our human reach would make having to deal with the hardships of life worth something.

3

MAIANA/FROM THE TOP

I'd fallen asleep. I wake to the sound of pouring rain. It's 9:20 p.m. and Mom and Dad are still not back yet. The TV is the only source of light in the house. Nickelodeon turned into Nick at Night and *The Fresh Prince of Bel Air* was playing—too old for me. I switched it to Disney and *Sister, Sister* is on. Now that's my jam. I turn on some lights because I'm very afraid of the dark. Whenever Mom and Dad get home this late I tend to get angry at them. Like, they should know how afraid I am of being by myself at night! God, why can't they just care? Why can't they just be here for me? I don't want to call them because I don't want to be a bother. They wouldn't come home sooner anyway. I repeat in my head that everything is okay. I make sure the outside doors are locked and every inside door is open at all times so that any intruders would have nowhere to hide. But why do I have to be the one to make myself feel secure and safe? They don't care what happens to me.

I start to whimper a little. I want to turn on the outside lights but it is so dark and I am scared that once they're on I'll see a taotaomo'na. Or a murderer.

I can't take it anymore. I pick up the phone and dial Dad's cell phone. I untangle the phone cord so that it could reach the kitchen's window so that I can stare out and keep watch for myself. He doesn't answer. I dial Mom's.

"Mom? When are you guys going to be home?"

She tells me they are waiting for the rain to settle a bit so that they can walk out to the car, but that it's okay because she's bringing back her leftovers from lunch—a whole adult size plate of spaghetti, my favorite food which she barely ate—from King's, my favorite restaurant.

"Can't you just run to the car? I'm scared."

She tells me that I'll be okay and that they will be home soon and aren't I "so lucky" for staying up late waiting for my favorite food.

"Can you stay on the phone with me at least?"

Of course, the answer is no. She says she will call back in a few minutes to check on me. "Forget it. I'll be fine," I say, not trying to mask my attitude in the slightest. "Just try to hurry."

Mom and Dad tell me they love me and to "just watch some TV." Yeah. Let the TV babysit me.

So I continue watching *Sister, Sister* and I start to get hungry again thinking of spaghetti. I *love* spaghetti if I hadn't already made that abundantly clear. I guess just another episode or two and then they'll be home in no time. Not long after I get comfortable on the couch again, the power flickers. "Nooo." Every scary story I'd ever heard comes flooding into my mind. The ones about someone walking into the jungle and coming out with bruises from the taotaomo'na. Or the ones about someone seeing

The White Lady on that road where people always claim to see her at night and smelling her strong scent of plumerias where plumerias are not present. Or the ones of duendes abducting children, making them sick, eating them, turning them into pebbles, or pulling tricks on people.

I need a flashlight. I remember they are in the bathroom underneath the sink. Dad said it was good to keep them in the central-most part of the house; that way, no matter where you were in the house, you'd more than likely be near them. I stand and slowly walk to the hallway. I hate hallways. All the lights are on. I have nothing to be scared of. And I have to be quick before the power goes—

The power fluctuates again. But this time, the lights don't come back on like the last time... except the hallway light. The very one I'm staring into. Somehow, I find that scarier. I should hurry before this goes off, too.

My legs are moving, just not as fast as I want them to.

I walk...

And walk... And walk...

And as I walk past my bedroom to my right, I notice how dark it is without turning to actually look. It's just black. I don't want to look. And I really don't *mean* to. I turn my head accidentally, thinking that I'll see nothing but complete darkness... and I see yellow dots sprinkled in the dark.

"Oh no," I say more casually than my brain does. "No, no, no." I book it to the bathroom and lock myself in. I rummage through the cabinet frantically, feeling around for the flashlight. Thankfully, it's not too hard to find, and I have it turned on immediately. I decide to sit on the floor by the shower and catch my breath, not knowing what else to do.

Where my flashlight is pointing is all I can see, and something is there. It takes off quickly from the spotlight of the flashlight. I don't get a good look at it, but quickly realize the only place it can run is to the other side of the bathroom... exactly where I am.

I scream. I lunge straight for the door and run out. When I step back into the hallway, I'm scared to pass my room but I have to. As I run past, my eyes darted into my room again. This time there are more floating, glowing eyes staring at me. Still screaming, I run out of the house and into the dark car port. I point the flashlight through the screen door but I can't see anything through it.

Outside, I feel exposed. I feel like something is going to grab me at any moment. I start to cry aloud. Moments later, bright lights wash over me. They get bigger and brighter very quickly and I don't move at all. My legs are shaking. If I move, I'll fall.

Car doors open and close. Mom and Dad come running up to me, asking what is wrong. Dad grabs a baseball bat from the sports bin that sits outside and scopes out the house. Mom picks me up like I am a toddler and rushes back inside the car. She locks the doors. She's on her cell phone calling the police. I'm still crying. I haven't cried like this in a long time. I've been so angry and upset for so long that I've forgotten how soft and vulnerable and baby-like it is to cry with everything you have. All the terror in me is releasing. My tears soak my shirt. I'm a baby. I'm the soft spot of a baby's head. I've got no hard exterior.

Through my whimpering I say to Mom, "I was all alone!"

She doesn't look at me. Focusing on the house, waiting for Dad or an intruder to run out, she says, "Neni, it's okay. We were only a few minutes away."

······

Mom and Dad keep asking me if I want to stay home from school since I was up late and clearly traumatized. I want to go, though. Especially because I don't feel safe at home. One of them would have to stay with me, of course, and I know they stress out when they miss work, but I think I also want to be able to tell Isa about what happened.

I have always wanted to be someone with an interesting scary story but... who would even believe this? Saying it out loud sounded like I was making it up. It just sounds so unbelievable. But last night... I know it was real and the next time something goes bump in the night, that might be real, too.

"Woah," Isa exclaims, "and you were there all by yourself? Oh, my gosh. I would have peed myself."

"I'd never been so scared in my life. Maybe in the bathroom when I tried to do Bloody Mary by myself at home, but that turned out uneventful."

We take our trays from Ms. Mary. "Si yu'us ma'åse, Ms. Mary."

"Ms. Mary! There was a monster in Maiana's house yesterday!"

"Oh really? That sounds awful." She adds another corn dog to our trays with a wink. "For your monster troubles, girls."

Once seated, we smile about our extra dogs, feeling special, and eat our meal in silence. Then Isa breaks out *The Secret Garden*.

"Oh dang, I forgot your book! Oh, and I also forgot to read it. Sorry."

"Psh, it's fine. I'm surprised you even came to school at all. I would have stayed home. Not because I was still scared, but just to skip school."

The end-of-lunch bell rings and everyone scatters to go to their class. Isa and I go our separate ways, but I notice that she is going out through the cafeteria door that is farthest from us. I quickly see that it's because the Tweedles are going out this way. She wants to avoid them. Why do these people have to exist? Why? What is so hard about just... being nice? Living in harmony with one another? Or just minding your own business?

I spend the rest of the school day cursing Nevaeh and Junie for being the way they are. Perhaps I just want something to obsess over that isn't about last night, however, when the bus is about to drop me off, I can no longer keep it out of my mind.

I step off the bus and know it's time to walk up the steep road. It looks longer than usual. The trees look thicker. I want to run the rest of the way but can't. Running up this slope would be like trying to run in water. I only need to focus on moving one foot in front of the other. I stare at my feet and sing a song to myself so I don't hear the jungle beyond the street's edge.

> *"Lights on the ocean means,*
> *Fairies in motion.*
> *I'm feeling emotion,*
> *It feels like devotion*

To me."

I hear a rustling somewhere beside me. It has to be lizards. Or cockroaches. Or birds trying to find food within the jungle. Only, the sounds are definitely caused by something larger. I sing louder.

"This island is talking

To me.

It's in the waves crashing."

I try to sing my heart out, hoping that my own song could help me in this moment of fear. Is there something out here? Following me? I stop walking to see if it will continue.

It doesn't.

I take a few steps forward.

It follows.

I immediately start walking backwards to trick it.

I shout-sing on my continued walk. But I have to start all over because the song isn't finished yet.

"LIGHTS ON THE OCEAN MEANS,

FAIRIES IN MOTION.

I'M FEELING EMOTION,

IT FEELS LIKE DEVOTION!"

I shout the lyrics with shallow breaths.

"TO ME... THIS ISLAND IS... TALKING," I suck in air, *"TO ME!"*

It's still following.

Fuck it. I start running. "Ahhh!"

I don't stop screaming until I lock myself in my bedroom. Why did I lock myself in my bedroom? I don't know! I need to get to the phone. I need to call Mom or Dad to let them know I made it home and also to ask if one of them could come home early.

It is dead silent in the entire house. My breathing sounds extremely loud. I can hear ringing in my ears, too, and I have no way of lowering the noise in my head. I feel like it can hear me—whatever *it* is.

A few minutes pass and my breathing is finally calm. I open the door a little to make sure the coast is clear.

I crack my door open very slowly, but holy creaking. That does not help my stealth at all. Dad was supposed to oil every door a long time ago. Thanks, Dad! If I die, just know it was you that gave me away. I see the phone on the wall down the hall, but not the receiver. My eyes follow the cord. It is being dragged on the floor by someone, or something, to the right. They're out of my view. The cord is moving though, bouncing up and down slightly above the floor as if a baby is playing with it. I don't want to leave the room. What the hell do I do now? I reflexively look to the window, even though I know I can't escape because it's barred.

I'm stuck.

Fine. I do my homework. That is until I heard my name.

"Maiana? Maiana, are you here?"

I shoot up from my bed. "Mom!" I run out of my bedroom but stay in the hallway.

"Mom?" I wait for her to find me standing there, but she never comes. And she doesn't call for me again. I know I heard her. She was loud and echoed through the quiet house. I walk slowly to the end of the hallway. Look to my right, where the kitchen and entrance to the house is. She is not there. I look to the left, where the living room is. Not there either. The phone receiver is still on the floor. I figure that while I'm out here I could call somebody.

Slowly, I walk over to pick it up. But the closer I'm getting, the more I can hear something coming through it. I put it to my ear.

It's Mom's voice. She's having a full on conversation.

"Hello?" I answer. She is talking with someone. "Mom? Can you hear me?"

I hear another voice.

" —and then you guys came home and then I was okay. I think it was just the rain that scared me. I was being silly and should stop being afraid of the rain. I was such a baby because I'm about to be ten and I understand that—"

Holy shit! That's my voice! That is *my* voice! I accidentally drop the receiver as if it burned my hand, but who the fuck is that talking in my voice? I quickly pick up the phone and slam it on the hang-up buttons. I pick it up and they are still talking. I slam it three more times to make damn sure that it hangs up but the voices are laughing aggressively now, to the point that neither sound human anymore. I begin to wonder whether the voices are laughing at me or their conversation, but I can't tell.

The phone is no use. I turn to escape through the front door, but right outside the screen door is a dark figure. A small, dark figure. Not a person. I'd be able to see a person through the mesh of the screen door. No, this is... impersonating a small person but missing all the physical features. It's staring in. Staring at me. Although I cannot see any indication of eyes, I know it is watching me. I'm frozen. It sure as hell doesn't feel friendly. Not after hearing it take my voice on the phone. That was this thing... right? All I can do is be grateful that it isn't coming after me but I don't want it watching me another second. I turn calmly and walk back to my room. I close the door ever so gently and continue working on my homework, trying to convince myself that this is all in my underdeveloped, over-imaginative brain.

When Mom and Dad finally come home—thank goodness it was still daylight—I had long since started reading a book. I read out loud so as not to hear a single thing that may or may not be happening outside my bedroom door. Whenever I read out loud, I read like a newscaster. Don't ask me why, but as soon as I had focused on my newscasting voice it did help me a little bit to forget about my fear. But when I hear Mom and Dad's voices having a conversation with each other I know it couldn't be another trick. I'm so happy and so hopeful that it is actually them that I ran out, caution be damned.

I ran to Mom and hugged her tight. No words. Their conversation completely pauses and they share a concerned look. She picks me up again like I am a toddler and I have a tight koala-hold on her.

"Nen, what's wrong?" She rubs my head as she asks, "Did it happen again?"

I really don't want to bring up monsters again so I say nothing. Mom stays right beside me for the rest of the night. We eat dinner with her arm around me. She does a newspaper crossword puzzle in the bathroom as I take a shower. She watches *Sister, Sister* with me on the couch. And she tucks me into bed.

"Mom?" She is silent, patiently waiting for me to say something. Patiently. Maybe she really does care about me. "I'm sorry. I'm sorry for scaring you."

She gives me a look as if I'm acting ridiculous and scooches me over so she can lay next to me. "I'm sorry you have to be home alone for a few hours. If I never had to work so that I could be with you all the time, I would. I'm also sorry you feel afraid sometimes."

There it is. My apology.

I love this woman.

I snuggle into her shoulder. I feel so comfortable in the safety of her presence that I quickly fall asleep.

4

MAIANA/AWFUL YELLOW EYES

I must have been asleep for a while. Mom is gone and the only source of light is from the full moon. My clock reads only 2:30 a.m. Why am I awake? I close my eyes to try to force myself back to sleep. Instead, I am wide awake with fear. I would love nothing more than to crawl into Mom and Dad's bed, but I'm terrified I'll see those awful yellow eyes on my way there.

I stare out of the window from my bed at the moon. I always find it soothing. Or at least it normally is. It doesn't work this time. So I just... simply... look away. And I shouldn't have. My eyes settle on those dreadful, floating, glowing eyes. I watch them closely. I seem to have stopped breathing, as if it could detect life, and if so I'm trying to be as lifeless as possible.

Without blinking, the eyes come closer. Closer they floated. The creature is about to step into the moonlight and my fear seems to inflate inside me. I know that whatever the light of the moon exposes, will cause all of my breath to release in the form of a scream.

In three... two... one.

It is a small... creature... thing. It's got rough dark brown skin, messy black hair, and long arms that are not proportionate to its body according to human anatomy standards. Its clothing looks like it's made from coconut husks.

"Ahhh!"

Within moments, Mom and Dad come running in, but when they turn the lights on, the eyes disappear.

"What's going on?" Dad demands, scanning the room.

Mom crouches by my bed and touches my leg, "What happened, nen? Bad dream?"

I am sitting in bed crying, with my back pressed against my wall. "Turn the light back off!" I shout. "Turn it off so you can see it! It's there! It's right over there! Hurry!"

It takes them a beat to hear me clearly in the chaos, but when they turn it off they see nothing. Nobody says anything. The light stays off, but Dad picks me up and they tell me I'll sleep with them tonight. They tuck me in between them and assure me that I must have had a bad dream. It couldn't possibly have been a dream. I most definitely was awake.

They fall back asleep in minutes. I can't.

Those eyes... They never look away from me. I watched them follow us into Mom and Dad's room. I watched them watch me get tucked in. The longer I stare back, the clearer I can see that the creature does have some features. Its eyes are a bit too big. Its mouth a bit too wide. Its skin as rough as a tree trunk. I gradually recognize what's happening.

I know what creature those awful yellow eyes belong to.

....

"Yup. That sounds like the duendes. They mess with children, adults can't see them, and I don't care how nice people try to make them sound in their stories, but they're freaky!"

"It was scary."

"What did your parents have to say?"

"Are you kidding? I didn't tell them what I thought it was. They don't believe in that stuff."

"What stuff? CHamoru legends?"

"Mhm."

"Well, why not? My parents do. They believe it all."

"Well, why? Do they know for a fact that it's real?"

"They always tell me it's better to assume they're real than to disrespect our ancestors and other presences that may have been here before us. I mean, there's a reason these stories have been passed down for generations, right?"

"Well, you could say the same thing for Mother Goose rhymes."

Isa looks at me like I'm ridiculous. "Mother Goose is not from here. Also, you're literally the one telling me some duende was in your house last night."

"Yeah. You got me there. So, you believe me?"

"Yeah, why not? My parents tell me they're real, you're telling me you saw one; I have to believe you. And I'd believe you anyway because, well, you're my best friend."

The warmth I always feel when I'm around her makes up for

the lack of warmth I feel from my parents sometimes. She gets me. She sees me. And not because she has to, but because I matter to her.

"I don't think you need to be scared of the duendes. If they wanted to hurt you, they would have done it already. Right?"

The thought of them wanting to hurt me scares me. Oh, God. What if that one duende comes back tonight? "Do you want to come over after school?"

She is excited and I can see she's already planning in her head how she's going to plead to her mom.

"You have to come over! I really don't want to be alone at the house! Pot fabot!" I put my hands together, almost begging.

"Well of course I'll come over!" She takes my hand and drags me out of the cafeteria.

I wait outside of the office while she goes to make her call. I don't have to ask my parents. They'll just be happy I'm socializing.

Oh, great. The Tweedles are coming this way. I turn away from them but it's too late.

They've spotted me. Ugh. They're walking up to me. This should be interesting.

"Oooh, did someone get in trouble? Is Miss Goody Two-Shoes finally one of us now?"

I laugh nervously, trying too hard at playing it cool. "No, I'm just waiting for Isa. She's calling her mom so she can come over after school." I curse myself for sounding so freaking nice.

Nevaeh whispers in Junie's ear and Junie whispers in Kimmy's ear and they laugh as they look at me. They're always laughing.

The fuck is always so funny to them? I wish so badly I could tell them to go get a personality and a sense of humor and then they can laugh at me all they want. But they're not funny. There is nothing funny about them or about me.

The laughing stops abruptly. "Oh hey, Napu," Nevaeh says sweetly.

"Hey, guys!" he says to all of us as he is on his way into the office. He pulls the door open, but before he walks through, he says, "Cool shirt," He points at me and continues through the doorway singing Britney Spears' *"Baby One More Time."*

Her eyes bore into mine. I know this look. Her brain is switching gears from plain mean to jealous. The other girls watch her watch me. She takes a deep and calming breath as she walks over to a plumeria shrub and picks one of the flowers. She takes my face in her hands and brushes my long, flat hair behind my ear and gently tucks the flower there. "Your shirt may be 'cool,' but your face is ugly. Keep a flower in your hair and then maybe we wouldn't want to vomit whenever we look at you."

As if that isn't enough to bruise my feelings, she let me know one more time. "God, you're so ugly."

I try to move my chin from her hand but she won't let me. She smiles wider at her physical control over me. She is delighted by the shame on my face. Just then, Isa walks out.

"Isa!" Nevaeh skips to the same plumeria shrub and picks one. "You get one, too!" She puts the beautiful yet tainted flower in my best friend's hair and the group walks away entertained.

"Uh, do I even want to know?"

I scowl at them, at all of them, as they walk away. I hate them.

And I hate myself for not standing up to Nevaeh, for myself or for Isa. My blood is boiling but it's my eyes that burn. "It's nothing. Well, nothing new, anyway." I take the plumeria out of my hair and stomp on it until it's ground into paste in the cement. Isa does the same.

I'm glad Isa is going to be home with me today. The fact that she isn't afraid to be at my house after last night tells me that either she isn't actually a believer, doesn't believe me, or she's as dumb as rocks. Or just a good friend.

Isa is a car rider, so she is having a lot of fun with all the attention she's getting from the kids who keep asking her what she's doing on their bus. She is happy to keep informing everyone that she is going to my house.

When we get off the bus, she shouts goodbyes to the ones poking their heads out of the windows waving at her. You know what? I think Isa might actually be the popular one. Not Nevaeh or her stooges. Huh. Go figure.

We watch the bus drive away until we can no longer hear the kids on the bus. We turn around and Isa gasps at the steep road.

"Oh, this freakin' road." She pretends to do leg stretches. "Okay then," she says as if she's about to set off on a long journey, "so, you were walking home when you heard something following you? You think you'll be followed again? Should we go into the jungle and see if we can find anything?"

"Don't get too excited. And don't be stupid either. We're not going looking for it in the jungle."

As soon as we got to my house, I put a pot of water on the stove to make ichiban for the both of us. She walks around my whole house exploring—she's nosy like that. She picks up the phone hoping to get some spooky action but all she got was the dial tone. We give our moms a call to let them know we made it home. While she wanders, I turn on the TV to SpongeBob. It's always on after school, without fail. I could honestly watch reruns of it forever. There's just something so comforting about it.

We sat on the floor at the coffee table to eat. Everything feels normal and eventually we break out *Bomberman* on the Sega. We only play for twenty minutes because Isa is horrendously bad at it. Next, we play cards. War lasted for about half an hour and in the middle of our game of Speed, Mom calls to ask me to make some rice before she and Dad get home. She also says that Isa could stay for dinner before we hang up.

Bang, bang, bang.

Isa and I jump, dropping the cards, and look toward the front door but the sound isn't coming from that direction.

Tap, tap, tap.

I quickly go to Isa and grab her arm, for safety in some way. We look at each other. We know exactly where the tapping is coming from. We run to the doorway of my bedroom and peek in. We see a hand tap on my window again. Whoever it is, they're trying to be slick to spook us.

"What do we do?" I whisper.

"Hmm. Let's see if we can see them."

We walk up to the window, careful not to be noticed, we look down and see Nevaeh, Junie, and Kimmy sitting on their butts leaning against the house. Laughing like idiots.

We retreat to hide in the hallway once more. "Man, they really have nothing better to do," I say, low.

Isa smiles.

"What?"

"Want to have some fun?"

I perk up, loving the sound of this. "What do you have in mind?"

We listen to their trail. Their stupid girl giggles travel from my room to the outside of Mom and Dad's bedroom window. They bang on it. While they are there Isa pulls me outside of the house. We spy on them, still banging on the window. Isa takes a small pebble and throws it at them and hides. My eyes go big with entertained shock. We can hear them asking each other what the hell that was. I throw a pebble at them when I have a clear opportunity.

The girls get up and laugh, clear to them that they have been caught. Without searching for us, they seem to be heading back to do whatever popular mean girls do. Isa and I go back inside to continue our SpongeBob marathon.

5

Isa/Who Wants Tea

"Want to have some fun?" I pick up some pebbles and throw them at the trio one by one, keeping myself hidden. Maiana laughs and throws some, too.

Finally, they run away. "I swear, they need to get a life."

Maiana and I talk about all the reasons why we hate Nevaeh until her parents come home. It takes her no time at all to make fried rice for dinner and it is the best thing I have eaten in a while. We barely eat fried rice in my house. We mostly have chicken. And this spam fried rice tastes like a million dollar meal.

When I get home, I run into my house telling Mom and Dad, practically begging them, to make it more often. They say if I brush my teeth right now and go to bed they will make it tomorrow. So I do, with a Barbie in hand. She sits on my sink and she watches me brush. I take her by the hand and walk to my room. "Okay, Barbie, this is yo—" she is no longer holding hands with me. I could swear I took her. I check the bathroom and she is not there.

Hmm.

I go back to my room and... there she is. Tucked into bed.

Head turned facing me at the door.

Huh.

"There you are... you sneaky little thing." I must have tucked her in and brushed my teeth without her. Yeah. I'm sure that's it.

My pink night light makes my bedroom feel soft and cozy. The sound of the trees blowing from the wind makes my eyes heavy. My tired body stretches and triggers a deep yawn. I'm ready for sleep to take me.

As soon as I shut my eyes, I find myself in the middle of my house. I don't know how or when I got here but I seem to be having a tea party with my Barbies and stuffed animals. I look in my cup and I've got chocolate milk.

I look around momentarily and shrug. No one else's cups are full. "Alright, who's next?" I fill up all of their cups—Tonya the tiger, Olivia the elephant, and Barbies one through four. I haven't named them yet. I place the teapot down and pick up my chocolate milk for a sip. I notice it's empty before I even bring it to my lips. Which is weird because it was just full.

I laugh, embarrassed in front of my party guests. "Oh, have I already drank my tea? How silly of me," knowing damn well I did not. What the hell is going on?

"You don't deserve what's coming to you."

"Who said that?" Mom and Dad are nowhere to be seen. I smile at my guests. "Okay, who said that?"

Nothing.

"Oh, come on. Don't be shy, ladies. We've been friends for years! Well, a couple of you are newer, but we're all basically old friends. So, who said that?" I feel uneasy and just want to know already.

They don't want to talk so I refill my cup and take a sip of the pretend tea.

"You don't deserve what's coming to you, Isa."

The hot air from the voice in my ear startles me and I practically fly sideways out of my chair and land on the floor. No one is around but someone *has* to be. I look around my house for a sign of anybody. Mom. Dad. Grandma. An auntie. An uncle. Some cousins could be playing a prank on me. But there is no one else.

I sit back down with my dolls. I drink my tea and I try to keep a conversation when I notice their heads are all turned to me. But somehow they're not looking at me.

They're looking behind me.

I turn to look, but I wake up before I can see who it is.

6

NEVAEH/NOBODY BUT YOU

"I bet they screamed," Kimmy says.

"I bet they cried!" Junie exclaims.

"I just like giving them shit. Those stupid bitches will learn to stop talking to Napu. He's *my* friend."

"And ours," Kimmy chimes.

"Kimmy, he only talks to you guys because you're friends with me. Which I'm fine with, of course." I swear, I always need to spell things out for these idiots. "Anyway, I can't wait to tell him about this. I think he'll find it funny."

The girls start to take the lead while I lag behind. I keep hearing footsteps. Or something... dragging? In the jungle? I'm not really sure.

Hmm... I see. They think they're being sneaky. Well, they don't know anything. I'll wait for them to get a little closer, then I'll show them what happens when they try to sneak up on me.

I walk slower until I feel like they're practically right beside me. I turn in the direction of the shuffling. "GOT—cha," I yell, but no one is here. I look all around the area where they should have been.

What the...

Junie and Kimmy are just watching me, waiting for me to catch up but... "Di—Did you guys see them? Where did they go?"

Oh, don't look at each other as if you don't know what I'm talking about! I know they've been hearing it this entire time, same as me.

"See who?" Junie says.

"Fucking forget it. I swear, you guys are useless."

••••••••••

I don't know how anybody could enjoy this. Putting weapons on these poor creatures, not knowing that they are to be purposefully agitated by one another for a game they won't ever win. The little knives on their little feet, they don't know that their kicking and thrashing will result in bloodshed and death of their own kind. They're forced to play a game where they win nothing, but their captors do. Again and again they'll play, as many times as they want because the stakes are not on them, but on the birds. If I ever want Dad to pay attention to me, I better get over it and speak his language. That's why he brings me with him. He doesn't try to get us to understand each other, he only wants *me* to understand *him*. This is a one-way street I live on and there's no place to U-turn.

There's nothing to understand except that these birds have no choice. What these loud people say goes. I can only relate with them to that extent. Dad likes that I am eager to come here with him but it's not for this agonizing sport.

I think Napu enjoys this as little as I do. His dad brings him because Napu just likes to be out of the house. At least that's what he's told me before. But I like to think that he just likes hanging out with me. Like this is just our thing. No friends to interrupt us.

He comes over and opens a small plastic bag. "Okay, Nevaeh... so we've got a spam sushi and hot cheetos. Which one do you want?"

He almost always brings me something but I blush anyway. I chose the spam sushi. I always have to put my nose to it and take a big whiff of the smell before opening it.

"You better stop doing that before someone calls you out for being weird."

"Nobody will ever know that I do that." Nobody but you, because you're the only one who I ever allow to really see me.

"One of these days I'll tell everyone how weird you really are."

I punch him playfully on the shoulder. We both laugh as we take our usual walk around Talofofo village as we eat our snacks.

Just us.

7

— · —

MAIANA/CREATION OF GOD

My alarm goes off. I played her words in my head over and over all night—*God, you're so ugly*—until I fell asleep. I just don't feel like dealing with her today. Mom comes into my room wondering why I'm not getting ready for school.

"Oh, don't tell me you're not feeling well. Come on. Get up."

I give her the sad puppy-dog eyes. She stares at me for quite a long time and I almost say 'fine, I'll go to school', until she broke first.

Sigh. "You know what? You look like you haven't gotten much sleep."

I quickly added that I really hadn't.

"Okay. I guess I could see if I could call in and stay home with you. But your butt better stay in bed today! And no TV! It's not a free day. This is a 'catch up on rest' day. Got it?"

I try to smile weakly so as not to express too much pleasure. Sucker.

But I was the sucker. All morning I'd heard shuffling in my closet, the place where monsters live. I obviously refuse to check it out myself and I don't want to bother Mom with my nonsense, but by noon I couldn't help my curiosity. She looks annoyed by the dumb request but she checks anyway. She opens it and asks if I'm satisfied. I am not. I see it—the duende.

"Can I be in the living room with you? Please?"

Mom looks in the closet where my eyes are glued. She put a finger on her temple because I'm such a headache. "Sure. Come on, it's time for lunch anyway." As I get out of bed the duende's eyes stay connected to my bed like I'm still in it. In the living room, I hear my name whispered and realize it followed me. I try not to look at it, not to give it any attention, thinking that if I ignore it long enough, it will eventually go away. The duende says my name every few minutes and ignoring it becomes hard. After almost two hours I finally dare to glance. It's holding something of mine and shakes it at me. A game called gonggi. A sort of Korean version of jacks.

I am realizing that the more I look at this duende, the less afraid I am of it. When I finally acknowledge its presence, it stops shaking the box of gonggi and tilts its head in response. Mom is on the phone with work in the kitchen. I cautiously reach out for the box. I throw the stonelike pieces onto the floor and play by myself to show the duende how to play. After a few rounds, I push the pieces to it. I whisper, "See? This is how you play," careful not to draw Mom's attention. The creature is trying to copy my hand movements of throwing it up and catching them atop its bark-like textured fingers.

"One by one you snatch them from the floor. And when you've got them all, you toss them out again and snatch them two by two and one." When Mom's conversation seems to quiet, I turn to make sure she's preoccupied. She is still turned away, just listening to the speaker for a moment. I return to the duende. "Next, you throw them all up and try to catch as many of the stones as you can atop your hand. However many you catch, those are your points you've earned. And then you do it again. One by one, two by two, catch your points." I look over the duende's face.

"Can you talk?" I whisper.

It doesn't answer me.

"Na'an hu si Maiana. Hayi na'an mu?" I ask.

Nothing.

I pointed to myself once more. "Na'an hu si Maiana." I pointed to itself, asking with forced patience. "Hayi na'an mu? What is your name? Do you speak CHamoru? English?"

Still nothing.

"I need to know what to call you."

Mom comes back for her Lifetime movie and the duende seems done playing. It walks in the direction of my room.

I gather the gonggi and store them back in the box. "I'll be right back. I'm going to put these away," I say to Mom. But by the time I get to my room the little creature is gone. I look everywhere. Mom and Dad's room, bathroom, closets. The duende left.

I can't keep calling you duende. You are a... a... You are an enkantao nina'hiyong—a magical creation of God that I get to experience.

You are magic.

You are... Atte.

8

ISA/A BITCHY THING

"I'm going to kill her," I slam closed *The Secret Garden* and stuff it in my bag as the bell to go to class is still ringing. I walk out of the cafeteria and Napu and Juan come to walk with me.

"Where's your partner in crime?" Juan asks.

"I guess she's not here today," I shrug.

Napu says, "Unless she's just late."

"Doubt it. Oh! I have a bone to pick with you. Tell your evil girlfriend to stop stalking us."

Napu throws his head back in surprise. "She's not my girl-friend."

"But she is a stalker," Juan jokes. "*Your* stalker."

"No, Juan, not just his! She followed us to Maiana's house! And she thought she was smart enough to scare us. Her and her two butt kissers. They were all banging around the house and then ran away like cowards! You know, I bet she only acts tough but she's really not. Why are you guys even friends with her?"

"My parents are friends with her dad, so I see her a lot outside of school."

"Yeah, but she's—she's—," I'm struggling to say it, " —a bitch."

Napu and Juan's eyes go wide.

"Oh shit! Miss Goody Two-Shoes," Juan says, eyes wide in real shock. "I can't believe your language!"

Napu doesn't laugh. "I know she can be a lot sometimes but she doesn't have... the best..."

I can't believe what I'm hearing! Napu! Making excuses for someone like Nevaeh? Is he kaduku?

Nevaeh bumps hard into my backpack, making it drop to the ground. "Oops. Sorry. That was a very *bitchy* thing to do."

I'm terrified that she might have heard me. What are the chances that that's just a coincidence?

"What, you want to hit me back? Go ahead. Or are you too much of a *coward?*"

Alright. Definitely not a coincidence.

Napu gets in between us. "Nev, stop. Just go to class."

Nevaeh smiles at his presence. "Napu, come walk me to class."

He looks like he wants to say no but just does what she wants. With an annoyed sigh and a pat on my back he says, "Fine. See you later, Isa."

Juan asks, "You think she heard you?" utterly oblivious to her evil taunts.

"Uh, no doy. And I'm lucky to still be alive."

I have the same thought hours later when school is out. I come out of the bathroom as students are rushing to the front of the school, about to head to the car pick-up zone when I hear something that doesn't sound right. A commotion that doesn't feel right.

I follow the sounds to a darkened pocket of the hallway behind the girls' bathroom. There's a girl on the ground. Nevaeh is standing over her.

"Hey, are you okay?" When the girl turns I recognize her to be a year younger than me. I help her up but my focus is on Nevaeh, who still has a smirk on her face.

The girl wipes her glossy eyes away and points to Nevaeh. "She—She took my necklace," she cries.

"Do you ride the bus or are you a car-rider?"

"Bus."

I turn the girl around and give her a little shove. "Go, before the buses leave. Look for me tomorrow. I'll have your necklace for you," I say with a reassuring smile.

The little girl is more than happy to leave.

I can't help but stare so sickeningly at Nevaeh. "What is wrong with you? She's younger than us! Smaller!"

"Wow. Isa, I didn't know you had the balls to speak to me that way! Ha! Good for you, girl!"

"Just give me the necklace," I demand, holding my hand out. My voice is brave but I'm trying so hard to keep my hand from visibly shaking.

Nevaeh rolls her eyes and tries to walk past me but I don't let her.

Tweedle doesn't like that. She looks slightly downward at me, neither of us backing down from this stare down. I'm staring with fear in my eyes. She's staring with daggers. "Isa, you're going to *move* and *let me* pass. *With* my new necklace."

Oh yeah? Let's see about that.

I don't know how much time has passed before she put her face so close to mine that I can feel her hot breath. *"Mooove."*

She tries to pass me once more, so I reach out for the necklace around her neck and then...

Pretend you're on an adventure.

··•••·•••··

We are staring at each other from across the table. Mom and Dad have this odd grin directed at me. Large eyes and the fakest smiles I've ever seen.

Thankfully the waitress comes. "Håfa adai! What would you like?"

They instantly snap out of that weird trance, their odd features disappear as they look and point at the menu and order, like normal.

"Isa, what do you want?"

Oh, um... I don't know. I feel like I hadn't had a moment to look at the menu, although my drink has already run low. But it doesn't really matter what I want to order because here at House of Chin Fe, it's family style. So they always get what they know I love anyway. Fried duck, white rice, stir fry noodles. I suppose what they are really asking is if there is anything else I want on top of what's already ordered for me and themselves.

"Calamari appetizer, pot fabot," I say to the nice waitress who retrieves the menus and leaves me with Mom and Dad who are back to staring at me with those ridiculous grins and large eyes.

"Are you guys okay?"

Nothing. Not even a blink.

"If you guys think you're being funny, you're not."

Still nothing.

"O—kaaay… I'm gonna go to the bathroom."

Their heads follow in my direction. I feel better once the bathroom door is closed. I don't actually need to go, I just want to get away from that for a moment. As I play around with the sink water I try to remember when they started acting so strangely. The last thing I remember is being at school. Nevaeh standing over me.

Pain.

How did we get here? *When* did we get here? Did we take Mom's car or Dad's? Where's grandma and Grace? We never go anywhere without Grace and she never wants to go anywhere without grandma. I suppose they're at the house together now. And grandma is probably feeding Grace her dinner by now. And I guess put her to bed shortly after. But what time is it? When did I change my clothes? What was my conversation like with grandma when she picked me up today?

My memory is fuzzy. Maybe because of that stupid brat Nevaeh and her beating up on me. She must have done some real damage to me. So much damage that I can't even see my parents right.

I comb through my hair with my fingers just to stall a little longer and then leave the bathroom. I see Mom and Dad chowing down already. Great, because I'm starving.

"So how was school today?" Dad asks.

"It was fine," I say through a full mouth.

"Anything interesting happen today?" Mom asks.

"No." A big fat lie.

They look at each other and put their utensils down. "That's a big fat lie, Isa," Mom's eyes bore into mine.

I stop eating for a moment, trying really hard to remember if I had already revealed anything about Nevaeh. It's really hard to recall for some reason.

"My daughter, a hero. How bad did it hurt, though? Were you embarrassed? Nobody helped you. Does that make you sad? Angry?"

"I don't know what you're talking about."

Mom laughs. "It's okay! I just want to know how she made you feel. I bet you want to get her back. I bet you want to hurt her, too."

Dad says, "She can't get away with this."

"He's right. She can't get away with this. She'll probably do it again."

Dad puts a fist on the table and leans toward me slightly. "She violated you! She hurt you! She made you look stupid!"

"I discovered that I would be who I need to be for others. Helping that girl made me see what my heart is made of. I'm not going to let her infect me with hate. I know who I am now. I mean, you guys are always telling me about how to grow and to be a good person! Didn't I do good?"

Dad says, "We want a daughter who knows what she does and doesn't deserve."

I don't know what to say. They're not talking like themselves.

Do I get her back?

Do I leave it alone?

Do I try to have a meaningful conversation with her to end this once and for all?

Should I tell the principal? A teacher?

Should I just avoid her for the rest of our lives?

Should I try to be friends with her?

Should I get even?

There's a commotion going on somewhere in the restaurant but I can't focus on that. Right now, I need to think of what to do.

Do I want to do what's right? What *is* right?

Do what's best for me? Which would be getting even, according to Mom and Dad.

Do I do what's mature and talk with her?

Do I go to a teacher or principal like what is so-called encouraged by the school?

The screaming doesn't stop. I finally bring myself out of my thoughts. Mom's smug demeanor suddenly changes to join in on the commotion.

I am the commotion.

"Isa! Isa, stop!" Mom screams at me with tears in her eyes. The other restaurant goers are looking at me as well.

I look down at myself. My left hand is stabbing my right hand with a fork.

Over. And over. And over.

I panic at the sight of the action I didn't know I was doing. I scream, too, because I can't get myself to stop. "I can't stop! I can't stop!" I shriek.

I feel pain in my hand, I guess, now that I'm seeing it.

Dad is the only one not freaking out. "You see? You are taking your anger out on yourself. What are you gonna do about it?"

I'm stabbing.

Stabbing.

Stabbing.

Blood splashes all over my hands. I may not have control over my hands but I have control over the rest of my body.

I jerk my body to the left letting myself fall out of the booth and onto the floor. When I hit the floor...

I woke up on the floor of my bedroom. I sit up against my bed and try to realize what had just happened. My hand hurts. My hand is red but not with blood. I'm holding a Barbie in my other hand. When my dream suddenly comes rushing back to me, I do the stabbing motion onto my hurt hand and the familiar movement reaffirms that it was all just a nightmare and I was "stabbing" my hand with my doll. Just a stupid doll. I just had my first ever nightmare.

I've soiled myself.

9

MAIANA/BITING BACK

We begin the Fanoghe CHamoru followed by the Inifresi. Once more, Nevaeh is at it again, making it obvious that she is whispering to Junie about me, and because they keep looking at me, others are also. Have these kids' parents never taught them that staring is rude? *The fuck?* I make eye contact with each one who doesn't look away.

Fuck you.

And fuck you.

And you too, Darlene, you A-Honor Roll piece of garbage. Too smart for the class material yet too dumb for some common sense. Someday someone is going to sock you in the face.

I want to shout at them to mind their own business. I can feel tears trying to pool in my eyes, so I look out the window to find something else to focus on.

Sometimes I imagine what would happen if I just escaped through the window and ran away. What would everyone do? Would they blame themselves? Would they blame each other? Would they be sad if I were gone? Truly, sometimes I wonder. If I did run away, how long would it be until people start to forget that I was missing? How long until the memory of what I looked like would fade? What would be their last memory of—

Wait... there's something out there. I squint my eyes to try to make out the form and before I can guess any sort of animal, it runs toward the window in three chilling seconds and, as if it pushes me, I fall backward.

The bang of my tripping from my chair and falling to the floor catches the attention of the whole class. I feel my face go beet red.

Atte?

At least half the class is laughing at me, and of course Nevaeh is laughing the loudest. Really, Ms. Flores? You're not going to tell them to stop? You're not going to tell Nevaeh that her laugh is not only out of line but obnoxious? I see we are going to have yet another day of just ignoring bad behavior.

"Maiana Champaco! We are not messing around today."

Except for mine. Thanks for calling me out like that, Ms. Flores. You're super good at your job.

I take my time getting back on my feet as I look out the window. I also take my time flipping my chair upright.

"Today, Miss Champaco," Ms. Flores says.

I sit down and tears begin to swell in my eyes from embarrassment. And of course Nevaeh can't just fuck off! She makes a cry-baby gesture at me. Others are still watching the two of us. I know they feel sorry for me, but hell, if you're not going to come to my rescue, can you at least pretend you're not watching?

When the lunch bell rings, I go straight to the bathroom. Isa is pretty quiet this morning and I don't feel like bringing up my troubles to her. I stay in a stall so I can compose myself, when I hear Nevaeh come in with Junie and Kimmy. My heart races. My whole body starts to shake. It's like they're following me! I want to scream. I'm desperate for an old-fashioned tantrum.

"Try this one."

"I like that one. Gimme that."

"Jeez, okay. Oh! That's pretty!"

"I want this one. I'mma keep it."

"Um no. You can't. My mom will notice it's gone. I'll be lucky if she doesn't even notice I touched her makeup."

"But look how pretty this is on me! Your mom doesn't need it anyway. She's old."

Jeez, you gotta be kidding. I put my face in my hands, unable to imagine that this bullshit is going to end anytime soon.

I perk back up when I realize they are speaking in hushed tones. I quietly get back off the toilet and put an ear against the stall door.

... necklace... girl... crying... Isa...

Isa? What about Isa? I turn my head to put my other ear against the door, and seeing Atte's face also up against the door startles me so badly that I scream and slip–I don't even want to know what the hell I slipped on—and my body slams against the stall wall.

Oh, come on! Again? My hideout is blown.

I hear the feet of the girls, spin around and approach my stall.

"What the hell? Who's in there?" Nevaeh demands.

All three girls bang on the stall door. They are never going to stop. So... very reluctantly, I unlock it. They swing the door open very slowly, as if savoring the anticipation, the same way one might while opening a Christmas gift.

Junie and Kimmy look as if their Christmas gift is not something they asked for. Nevaeh, on the other hand—her eyes become laser focused on mine—oh, she's savoring her Christmas gift. A corner of her mouth lifts into a frightening grin. I'm trapped in this tiny bathroom stall with three girls who hate me for no reason and I have no idea what they're planning to do with me. What *Nevaeh* is planning to do with me. I have no idea what this sick and twisted girl is capable of. God, help me!

"Maiana?" she says with a scary calmness. "Girl, you've been in here a while! Were you taking a shit? You were, weren't you? I can smell it."

I keep my mouth shut. I know better than to give her something else to react to.

She laughs before speaking again. "Man, you're just having a bad day, huh? So be honest. Tell me what you heard."

I don't move. Don't want to speak. Hoping that she'll get bored and go away. But that's only wishful thinking. I know she won't leave me alone. Not while she has this rare opportunity alone with me.

She comes into the stall and puts her arm around me, guiding me out of the stall like a scared stray dog. "What did you hear?"

"I didn't hear anything!"

"Kim, grab me a lipstick."

Kimmy holds it out to her with some hesitation.

"Tsk, hurry up!" Nevaeh reaches the rest of the way and snatches it from her.

"Do you like makeup? I think maybe you need some... extra

help with your face. Because you remember how ugly you are, right?"

I'm shake my head no. I want to plead with her not to go through with whatever she is about to do with that lipstick but no words come out. Whatever is about to happen, I know isn't going to be in my favor.

She takes hold of my face, grabbing me by the chin. She opens the lipstick and applies it to my lips and then turns my head so that I can see myself in the mirror. "See? That doesn't look so bad, right? A beautiful CHamorita. Well, as good as it's gonna get, anyway. What do you think, girls?" The girls don't know what to say. They look uncomfortable. "You're right! She *does* need more lipstick!"

She takes my face again and this time I try pulling away. The more I go against her, the harder her hold is. Her long and jagged nails are painful and create indents in my skin. A tear falls out of my left eye. "Atte," I say, scared to call out for him, but I'm desperate. "Atte. Atte, please."

The three of them look at each other, confused.

"Atte? Ha, what the hell is Atte?" Nevaeh scoffs. "Atte! Atte!" she mocks.

"I can see in the mirror that Junie and Kimmy are wondering if they should stop her. Kimmy speaks up as soon as they see her overdraw the lipstick on my top lip.

"Nevaeh, I think you should stop."

"Oh, shut up."

"I think you're going a bit too far."

"That's the point, stupid!"

"Not the lipstick! I mean with Maiana."

Nevaeh ignores her and laughs as she overdraws my bottom lip. I try to turn my head to see into one of the stalls where I think I see Atte lurking in the shadow of the stall. She turns me to the mirror again. I whimper at the horrific sight of myself. Tears pool for the second time today. If I'm humiliated now I can't imagine if she decides to drag me out of here for everyone to see.

Thankfully, she lets me go and I immediately try to wash it off. It seems like it's only smearing and not really coming off at all. I start rubbing harder in panic.

Nevaeh and Junie are laughing and Kimmy looks like she wants to help me, although she does not.

Several paper towels later I can see my skin again, but it's red from all the rubbing.

"It looks like she has a rash," Junie exclaims. That only makes Nevaeh laugh harder. She skips out of the bathroom leaving the three of us in an awkward silence. Surprise, surprise, she sticks a plumeria in my hair, taking her sweet time placing it just right.

"Okay, I'm done here. Let's go to lunch." As she walks out, Nevaeh stops Kimmy. "Oh no, not you. You want to be nice to her? You can stay here with your new friend."

Kimmy stands there momentarily stunned as her so-called friends walk out on her.

I start drying off my super red face. I feel awkward with Kimmy here, ditched by her own friends. I think about saying something to make her feel better but why should I care? Sure, she didn't care for this specific incident, but she's still an enabler.

"She took it too far," Kimmy mumbles.

Was that an apology? It feels like it wants to be one but—

" —it's not," Atte says at the same time I thought it.

Oh, now *you show up?*

I am startled by the deep raspy voice that is Atte's and I look between Atte and Kimmy. She takes notice of the slight change in my demeanor. She sees that nothing is beside her but she moves away anyway, yet my eyes are still following Atte, who is following Kimmy. My behavior is making her nervous but I can't look away. Atte had finally said something and is standing right here and not even Kimmy can see him.

"Maiana, what the heck are you looking at?" She looks all around herself with caution.

"What was Nevaeh saying about Isa?"

She looks down. "I'm not supposed to say."

"She's not gonna tell you," Atte taunts.

I keep looking between her and Atte. It's hard not to keep doing that.

She thinks I'm odd. I can see it. I can feel it. I don't blame her this time. I know she regrets trying to come to my rescue. She's thinking it wasn't worth feeling sorry for this weirdo to feel Nevaeh's wrath later.

"Stop fucking with me. And I can't tell you. She's my friend."

"Well, Isa is mine. And my friend's name came out of your friend's mouth. So just tell me what that was about." I wish I'd said this more threateningly.

As Kimmy comes up with excuse after excuse Atte chimes in. "I think you need to... trick her... into telling you. Yeah. That's the only way."

Without glancing at Atte I'm shaking my head no as discreetly as I can.

"Just a little... a little scare."

Kimmy is finally done talking. She's staring at the ground now, trying to make me feel sorry for her for Nevaeh being mean to her, too, that it's not just Isa. That she's just mean to everyone.

"A little terror, like what Isa felt yesterday!" Atte jumps up on the bathroom counter to get behind Kimmy. "You don't know what happened, but I do. And let me tell you, Kimmy and the other one—the jiggly one—yeah, they both laughed when the mean one told them about it."

"So that's why I can't tell you," Kimmy concludes.

"Just let me. Please? A little stab right... there," Atte says while holding a long claw-like nail mere centimeters away from Kimmy's eyeball.

"Kimmy, if you don't tell me you're gonna get hurt," I blurt.

She notices my wide eyes. She blinks. I'm barely breathing.

Her head tilts in bafflement. "Is that a threat, Champaco?"

"Three..."

"Kimmy..."

"...two..."

Kimmy sighs.

"...one."

"She beat her up, okay? I thought you might take the hint but I guess you really are that stupid."

I didn't know how to react about Isa, for one, and for two, another insult. The jabs—

" —keep on coming," Atte says again together with my

thoughts. "She did it. She spilled the beans! Too bad her time ran out. Boop!" Atte's claw taps her eyeball, though lightly, her lid reacts, closing shut with a little *"Ow"* escaping her.

As soon as I released my breath, thinking that that was all he was going to do, Atte bites her on the side through her shirt.

Her contorting face and scream has me panicking to flee the scene. As she runs out crying I hurryingly wet more paper towels for my face and leave. But I don't get far before I come face to face with Nevaeh.

She turns away from her distraught friend to look at me and says, "Well, well, well. It seems the quiet ones do bite back."

A small chuckle escapes me as I thought, *literally.*

10

MAIANA/JUST A PHASE

Mom and dad spend dinner talking about things that happened at work. They ask me how school was and when I say it was fine they don't try to dig for details, which obviously I'm glad for, however, it had been a terrible day and I haven't even been trying to hide it. So, they either don't want to know or just straight up don't have a single clue. Do I want them to try to figure me out? Maybe just a little bit. Do I actually want to talk with them about it? Absolutely not. But it would be nice to know that they notice things about me without having to leave emotional crumb trails.

I'm not laughing at their jokes or silliness or trying to include myself in the conversation, and I can see them communicating with each other through an exchange of glances. I'm guessing they are saying something along the lines of *What's her deal?* and *I don't know, but she has to knock off this attitude.* And since they are not being discreet with it, I roll my eyes. And no, I also am not being discreet about it.

Dad points his fork at me. "Ay, you better watch it."

I rolled my eyes a second time without realizing.

Dad's eyes shoot to Mom as if saying she better do something about her daughter.

"Nen, if you're going to give attitude, go to your room."

"I'm not trying to give attitude! I had a really bad day at school and—"

"Ay! Don't talk back to your mother! And what, having a bad day at school makes it okay to be disrespectful to us?" Dad retorts, doing such a good job disciplining me.

My mind goes blank. I don't know what to say. I don't know how to proceed to talk with them. I won't be able to get a word in. I'm rendered to silence.

Talk, but don't say anything seems to be the motto in this house.

I stomp my way to my room. I start to close the door really fast like I'm going to slam it, but right before the door touches the frame, I stop it and close it softly. I'm fuming! Why would they ask me about my day if they didn't even care? What is the point in that? To make themselves feel like they're doing what good parents do? Couldn't they have just ignored me, sitting there picking at my food?

My stomach growls. Yeah, I guess I wasn't exactly shoveling my food into my mouth tonight. Yet, I refuse to go back out there! I hate them! I hate that they didn't want to listen to me and I hate that I don't have any food in my belly! I! Hate! Them!

I stop pacing around my room when I hear them start talking about me. "Maiana has got to stop with this attitude thing," Dad says.

"It's fine," Mom assures him. "She's just going through a

phase.”

Attitude thing? A phase? I want to scream! What about them? Are *they* going through a phase of bad parenting? Or is who I really am all my fault—my being angry from getting bullied and getting in trouble from acting out in anger?

I'm nine! Somebody, guide me! I'm drowning in all these awful and confusing feelings and God forbid I spit out the water from my lungs!

I scream into my pillow and then I hold it up as if I'm going to slam it on my bed, but my hands bring it down ever so gently, ever so angry.

“So, what are you gonna do about it?” Atte asks.

I sniffle as I turn to see him stepping from the cracked window. “About what?”

“The smiley one and the loud one.”

“Nothing! What can I do? They don't listen to me sometimes! I can never do anything about anything!”

Atte laughs. It's deep and unsettling. “Maybe you are a stupid girl.”

I purse my lips. I can almost feel the steam release from my ears. “You better shut up.”

“No, see, you're not getting it.” He jumps onto my bed. “I can help you do something about it. You don't call me Atte for nothing.”

“Uh... um... like what?”

“Together, we could scare. We could demand. We could get you what you desire. Motherfucking respect.”

How did he—

"Yes, I know what you're thinking. Your thoughts scream so loudly sometimes that I had to creep out of the jungle to shut them up. But instead, I watched you like you watch your television. And I saw that poor little Maiana was all alone. Angry. And it made *me* angry. I had seen enough. They all deserve... *an eye for an eye*." He laughs at his own joke about what he did to Kimmy.

The eagerness in his eyes are telling. He's hungry. He wants this more than I do. Discomfort replaces my anger.

"I—I don't think I want to do anything about anything. That's not really what I meant. I want to... I don't know..." I attempt to reel him in as I reel in my own emotions.

"There's only so many times you can keep making yourself the bigger person while no one else is. At some point it's not you, but everyone else. If they refuse to see, then at least get even."

"I don't want to talk about this anymore, Atte."

He scoffs and right before my eyes he makes himself small. Then leaves through the crack of the opened window. I'm left in amazement.

I lay back on my bed and stare at the ceiling. All I see is black. I don't know how much time has passed but The Quiet Storm is not helping this time so I turn it off. Now, the silence is deafening. I'm warm. I throw my blanket off. There is a chill in the midnight air. I pull it back over me. I stick one foot out because I'm still warm. I put my pillow over my face for the coolness of the pillowcase. I take it back off because I can't breathe.

I need some air. And some answers.

Mom and Dad have long since been in bed. I want to go find Atte. I grab a flashlight from the bathroom cabinet and quietly make my way outside. I take the box of gonggi with me just in case.

I can hear the pumping of my heart as I walk through the dark stillness of my house. I swallow down my fear but even the air is making me feel like I should just go back to bed.

"Atte!" I whisper-shout. "I need to ask you about Isa!"

All I hear are crickets, frogs, and the occasional buzzing of a mosquito.

I shake the gonggi box. "We can play a game if you want!" I stare as deep into the jungle as I can. "Is anyone there?" I ask in a volume that is more to myself. I am suddenly scared to call attention to myself. I can't explain the awareness I feel, but I know I'm not alone, and I know that whatever is present isn't Atte. Standing right outside of the jungle looking in, something is staring back at me and I just can't see it.

"Guella yan guello, may I enter your land?" I step into the jungle. As soon as my foot lands on their soil, all the hairs on my body rise. I feel as if I have entered a different world, each foot planted in two worlds.

I dared my other foot to enter, still shaking the box of gonggi. I try to focus my vision ahead; I see the same bunch of yellow eyes that I had seen in my bedroom. Though I am headed in their direction, they are never closer, never farther. Without signs of movement they remain the exact same distance from me. It makes me wonder if I'm walking in place somehow. It is extremely disorienting and makes me feel nauseous.

"Hello? Uh, my name is Maiana Champaco. I am looking for Atte. He's my friend."

Shouldn't I have made it to the other side by now? How is this possible?

"Little Maiana, what a surprise," Atte says, but not at all actually surprised. "How did you get in here?"

The question confuses me. "Uh... I don't know. I just walked."

"Yes, but you don't understand what you've walked into," Atte says as he walks a lap around me. "You have no idea where you really are. Allow me to show you around."

I look behind and try to remember how far into this weird jungle I am. I'm nervous being here and I don't want to lose my way. Now that I've found Atte I don't really want to go any further. He makes himself half my height as he continues to circle around me and it reminds me that the duendes have abilities that I need to be careful of. "Uh, I think I'm good here. I can't sleep and I wanted to ask about Isa. You said you know. I want to know."

"No. Here is not good. I've got a better place to go. A place you wouldn't believe. Anyway, you're already farther away from home than you think. What's a little farther?"

Before I can grasp what he means, Atte is nudging me forward. While he talks, I can't gather the words to express my concern and why. There are too many distractions. I feel like there are other things lurking in the dark around me and I know they can't be other duendes because there are no eyes. Just rustling of the grass and crunching of pebbles.

We arrive at a land that has nothing but a huge hut sitting on giant latte stones in the center, the kind you see in CHamoru history textbooks, but bigger. A huge hut sitting on giant latte stones.

"This is unreal! It's incredible. What is this place?" I start walking toward this fun-looking magical hut when I see someone, a woman, exit. I stop and stare with complete horror. Her skin is as pale as chalk. Her eyes sunken, droopy, defeated. Her hair is long and all over her shoulders and face, but the most unnerving thing about her was that it is easy to confuse the dark veins that show through her skin with her hair. I scream in horror and turn to run away without a second thought, but Atte stands in my way.

"What is this place?" he repeats me. This place is your future! This place is where you end up!" He turns me around and points to the woman. "Don't be afraid. That's you."

I'm filled with dread and I push him away. I run for home, unsettled that I can see through the dim light of the moon better than when I'd entered. I don't even realize when I reach the exit of the jungle until it feels like I am spat out, shoved out by some pressure. Like some kind of invisible hand or gust of wind on my back causes me to fall onto the pavement, back at the steep road once again.

I quickly get to my feet and glare at the jungle as if it's going to somehow pick me up and stick me back in there! First, my voice was copied, and now I'm to believe that *that* is my future self? I think not! I think *absolutely* not! I will never step foot in this jungle ever again!

11

Isa/Not Safe Anywhere

The necklace made it back to the hands of Nevaeh's little victim. I thought standing up for what is right was supposed to feel good. I'm not even myself today. I'm filled with embarrassment. Embarrassed by Nevaeh and Mom and Dad's discovery of my morning accident. I feel bad about not talking with Maiana very much. She keeps asking me what is wrong. She keeps saying she knows it's got something to do with the Tweedles. When I wouldn't answer, she started talking about her duende friend and how she named him Atte. I tried to seem interested but I can't get myself to pretend.

I'm thinking a lot about how I deserve to be treated. *You don't deserve what's coming to you.* I want to ask that voice in my head if there is something else coming to me that I don't deserve. But that's stupid, right? I'd only be asking myself. These are my own thoughts, so maybe I do want some sort of revenge. Maybe I do want something bad to happen to her. Maybe I'm not as innocent and strong as I thought.

I feel like I've got a devil on my shoulder and an angel on the other, like in cartoons. Is this a test? Is the universe testing me?

Is God? Am I testing myself?

I like passing tests.

I guess that settles it. I'm going to be the bigger person. My feelings are more hurt than my body.

That thought feels familiar.

I've said that in my nightmare.

I pray that my nightmares won't leak into my real life. I wouldn't survive it.

··•·•····

It's Friday and Mom and Dad want to take me to my favorite restaurant for dinner.

House of Chin Fe.

"I don't want to go there," I tell them. "I don't want to go there *ever*."

They are confused about my sudden change of heart, but I don't bother to explain. I don't know where I would start even if I did. Would I start with how Nevaeh beat me up? My weird dreams? My thoughts of harming Nevaeh, and possibly myself?

I want to be alone but I don't want to go to my room. I let mom and dad know that I'm going outside to pick some mango. Grace wobbles behind me, following.

Plastic bag in hand, I go to our big mango tree and scan the ground for fallen ones. I feel them if they're soft or hard, and inspect if they've been eaten by stray animals or attacked by bugs. I put six good ones in the bag when I hear Grace repeating the word "bad."

"No, Grace, these are the good ones," I say, still scouring.

"Bad. That's bad. I don't like it. I don't want it," she complains.

"Ughhh, don't eat it then, nai," I shoot back.

"Stop! Stop!" she points with a demanding finger.

I turn around to address the annoying behavior. "Grace, can you please qui—" She is pointing at something in the mango tree. Why would she be talking to something in the mango tree? "Grace, who are you talking to?" I don't look. I want to hear what she has to say first. Also, I really don't want to look.

Whatever it is, she gives it a mean mugging. "I don't like that thing. Stop looking at me!" She crosses her arms.

I suck air in deeply and prepare for something awful. At first glance I don't see anything. But as I focus more on the shadows, looking deeper, I see yellow. It's not the yellows of a mango. What are they? I take two steps closer and tilt my head. I extend my neck as if that will bring me closer for a better look. Without breaking my gaze with the yellow eyes, I bend down slowly and reach for a mango to throw into the tree. But then the yellow disappears and reappears I froze. That was a blink. The mango drops from my hand and I back away, taking Grace's hand.

"Come on. That's enough mango. Go. Go!"

We rush back into the house and it's like Grace has already forgotten about it.

....

Camping is sprung on me. If I knew we were going camping this weekend, I would have invited Maiana. I bet this is because of me. I know I haven't been myself lately and I'm sure they have noticed. Maybe I just gotta get used to these nightmares. Nevaeh did this. I only started having them since... she...

"Ugh! I can't get this stupid tent up! Can somebody help me out?"

Dad, in his cheerful tone, tells me that he wants me to try to put it up all by myself.

Okay. Okay, fine. I close my eyes. I take a deep breath, just like Mom and Dad have always told me whenever I start to feel myself getting angry.

Fine. This is supposed to be a fun weekend. I can't allow myself to ruin everyone's weekend.

"Hey! Looks like you could use some help!"

"Maiana? Maiana!"

Inviting Maiana to surprise me is not something I would have expected from Mom and Dad. I can feel the dark cloud that has hovered over me these past few days run away from sunshine that is my best friend. And she helps me put the tent together.

Fishing with Mom and Dad is so relaxing. As I lie in the swaying boat reading *The Secret Garden*, Maiana breaks out in song. Mom and Dad are compelled to sing along and all seems right in the world—at this moment in time at least. I'm scared to sleep, though. Making up the sleeping bags is making me nervous. What happens when I have another nightmare? My first odd dream, I fell out of my bed. My first nightmare, I was stabbing my hand with a doll. It would be really embarrassing if I woke up Maiana by doing something in my sleep. And speaking of embarrassing... *Please don't let me wet the bed tonight.*

"You asleep?" Maiana asks.

I sigh. "I'm trying."

12

— · —

MAIANA/THE LEGEND IS REAL

The smell of bacon, eggs, and rice wafts into my room. They know I've not forgotten about last night and I know this is their attempt to lure me out. Well, it's not going to work this time. My heart was hurting in a different way than it ever had and they didn't even try to understand. My belly growls in agreement.

I hear footsteps coming down the hall. You know what? Bring it! Today, I'm prepared for war!

Mom opens my door. Figures. Dad never says a word to me until Mom's got me in a better mood. "Morning! Food's ready!"

"Not hungry."

"No? Well, you'll want to come out anyway. We've got a surprise for you."

Oh, jeez. This is probably one of her tricks where she tells me I have a surprise. But, surprise! You've got a new "big girl chore!" And then it becomes a funny wholesome story to tell their friends and other family.

I walk to the kitchen, not upset, but not happy either. Mom makes me a plate and I sigh my thanks. I scarf it down nonetheless.

"Nen, guess what." Oh. He's actually speaking to me.

"You're going camping with your friend!" Mom finishes for him.

This is definitely surprising. "What?"

Isa's Mom called to ask if you'd want to join them on their camping weekend. She said Isa is a bit under the weather or something and by having you accompany them would probably cheer her up. And... maybe cheer you up, too." Mom is smiling at me with hope in her eyes. Of course I want to go, but wouldn't I rather hear the words of an apology? Or am I going to let them sucker me into getting over it?

Dad says, "There will be fishing, grilling, and it's a sleepover. Isn't that fun? Don't you want to go? We thought you'd be excited."

I don't look at them, holding my grudge.

Dad stretches, getting up from the dining chair. "I mean, if you don't feel like it, we could always call them back and tell them you don't—"

"No!" I cave. "I want to go!" I shovel the rest of my breakfast down as they exchange winning glances with each other. I express enthusiasm and brighten my mood for them. There. Moving on. I'll just add this to my list of silent apologies.

As we pull up into the parking lot of Ipan Beach I can see Isa struggling to put up her tent beside her parents'. The three of us unload from the car and while Isa's parents greet us I see her trying to make out who her parents are chatting with. I run over to her.

"Hey! Looks like you could use some help!"

"Maiana? Maiana!"

"Surprise!" I say with a grin.

She laughs and gives me a great big hug. "What are you doing here? I didn't know we were camping today and was sad I didn't get a chance to tell you."

"They called this morning to surprise you."

"Well, I am surprised!" She gives me another hug.

I grab a pole and slide it into an appropriate-looking slot. "Why are you doing this by yourself, anyway? How come they're not helping?"

Isa rolls her eyes. "They think they *are* helping me by making me figure it out on my own. You know how they are."

Yeah. I do know. They care about her independence. They are always pushing her in ways that will benefit her in the long run.

After we got the tent set up, we went out on the ocean to fish. Well, Isa's parents fish while Isa and I read— *The Secret Garden* and *The Giving Tree*. Isa is about halfway done with the ginormous thing while I finish this teeny tiny one. It really is a great book. Probably better than my contribution. While she continues reading and the adults continue fishing, I lay back and stare at the thick clouds.

"Lights on the ocean means

Fairies on motion.

I'm feeling emotion.

It feels like devotion

To me.

This island is talking

To me.

It's in the waves crashing."

"Nen, that was very nice. What is that song?" Isa's mom asks.

"I don't know what I'm gonna call it yet."

Her eyes light up. "Oh, you wrote that yourself?"

"Mhm."

"Mom, she wants to be a writer when she grows up. She's really good at it!"

Her parents want to sing along even though I told them that that's all the words to it so far. A few minutes later, it became our sea shanty.

"Lights on the ocean means

Fairies in motion.

I'm feeling emotion.

It feels like devotion

To me.

This island is talking

To me.

It's in the waves crashing!"

Over the next hour, they caught five fish and found two Dungeness crabs. After we bring our harvest back, Isa and I swim while they prepare dinner. Scale the fish, clean the crabs, and get a pot of red rice going. Isa and I play out the legend of Sirena. Isa is Sirena who turns into a mermaid while I play her mother who never wants her to be in the water. I don't exactly know how to play the role of Sirena's mother while Isa is out swimming farther and farther away, so I just look for some rocks to throw as far as I can.

"Sirena! Ai, Sirena, come back!" I scream ridiculously. "Oh, my daughter! I hope fishermen don't find you first! They'll cook you up like fish!" and other such nonsense. It's quite entertaining, actually. Once in a while, I'll see her parents pointing and laughing at me, also entertained.

When dinner is finally ready, we rinse ourselves and change into fresh clothes. We are starving. Isa and I each get a fish and red rice, and let us have the crabs. As we eat we watch as the sun's light disappears from the sky. I watch the thousands of imaginary little fairies dance atop the rippling water. When the stars appear, we are all mesmerized. If I could not sleep so that I could stare into the night sky until the pinks of the rising sun showed, I would.

After dinner, Isa's dad drives down the road to the store for some snacks—several bags of chips. They allow us to snack on junk until it's time for bed. The sleeping bag is cozy. The ocean—oh, the ocean waves—there's something so different about it when you get to sleep with it.

"Man, what a good day. I can't believe you guys do this all the time. Doing this would tire Mom and Dad out for months. I wish I could convince them to do this."

At a certain point, I realize that I have been doing most of the talking. "You asleep?"

She turns to me in her sleeping bag. "I'm trying."

Hmm. "What's wrong?"

"What? Nothing."

"You were quiet at school and you've been less talkative today. It's not like you to be this quiet."

Isa exhales an audible breath. She shakes her head, collecting her thoughts. "I was just trying to get a necklace that she took from some younger girl. She shoved me. Stepped on me so I couldn't get up. Spat on me."

My jaw is on the floor. I'm speechless and in disbelief. She didn't have to say who; But I know.

"She's not done yet," Atte says, suddenly beside her.

Her tears come suddenly, falling heavily, one after another as she chokes out the next part.

"She kicked me, and kicked me, and then kicked me one more time. All in the same spot on my side." She throws her face into her pillow so her parents can't hear her sobs. "At least it seemed like she held back but, Maiana, I've never felt so violated. I've never *been* so violated."

As she cries into my arms, Atte says, "What are you going to do about it? Your sweet little friend has been harmed."

"And... I... think I..." She hides her face with her hands as she says, "Don't laugh when I say this."

"I won't."

"I think I started wetting the bed because of this."

That's not at all what I was expecting, but my stupid, immature self smirked a little.

"Maiana!" She pounds a fist on her sleeping bag.

"I didn't mean that. You know I didn't mean that. I just—wasn't expecting that. I'm sorry. Keep going."

She drops into her sleeping bag with her pillow over her face, crying.

I rush to her side and cuddle her.

Atte says, "What are you going to do about it? Your sweet little friend has been harmed."

All Isa ever wants to do is play pretend. All she knows is to be kind. All she needs is protection. I'll protect her.

"*We'll* protect her," Atte beams.

·····•·•····

The beach is lively today with more kids, pet dogs, and island music as other beach goers barbeque. Isa is sharing her Barbies with a younger girl who looks around the same age as her little sister, Grace. She and their grandma had better things to do; that's what Isa's parents said. I absolutely don't want anything to do with playing with dolls so I tell her I'll be back, looking for something else to entertain myself. Since we used up our collection of shells from yesterday, I guess I'll start a new collection. I find six fairly big shells before I decide to search in the shallow water.

I pretend I'm on my own adventure looking for treasures in the depths of the ocean. As I dip in and out of the water, Atte's words replay in my head over and over again. *We'll protect her.* I've never heard of a duende protecting anything or anyone. Have the legends got them all wrong? Can't be. Atte is fully capable of harm. Does he want to do harm to Nevaeh? Does he really want to keep Isa safe? Why would a duende care? Is it because Isa is my friend and he's my friend, too? None of this makes much sense. Though, I'd be lying if I said I wasn't interested.

I push myself up to the surface of the water. The salt burns my eyes. It always takes some getting used to before feeling like the warm water is worth the burn. Once my eyes stop burning and readjust, I find myself far from where I was just moments ago. I see how far away the shore is and panic sets in. It sets in hard.

"Oh my God!" I scream while keeping myself afloat. "Help! Help!"

"Calm down, little Maiana. You're not going to drown."

When I start to feel the truth of that I finally calm down. But now I'm annoyed. "Why do you keep doing this?" I shout angrily.

"Do what? Make things more interesting? More fun?" He grins.

"You're always scaring the hell out of me! What's up with that? And it's not fun at all!"

He's got the boat. Isa's parents' boat. How did he row it out here in mere seconds? I suddenly remember how quickly he ran up to my classroom window. It's unnerving that the duendes have the ability to do odd things that go unnoticed.

"Well then, why don't you tell me what your idea of fun is? Knowing what you know."

"Huh? What are you talking about?"

"You know what I'm talking about. Just say it. And I can make it real."

I don't... What does he want me to say?

He's watching me contemplatively.

Isa. We'll *protect her.*

"I know what you want. Let it roll off your tongue. See how it feels."

I... want... "Revenge."

Atte howls in laughter. "There she is. Little Maiana, thinking with her big girl feelings. Tell me, what kind of revenge?"

"Uh… I don't know." I'm floating in the water, paddling with my hands even though I don't need to, but it's uncomfortable asking someone to do something bad to someone. I know it's wrong. Yet, all I want to think about is what I can do with my hands.

"Tell me."

"I don't know."

"Tell me! She kicked your friend. Stepped on her. Laughed at her! Laughed at *you*! She put hands on both of you and you're telling me that you don't know what you want to happen to her? Pathetic. You're pathetic!"

"I don't know! I don't want to know. Just do *something*! Anything! Do something good. Make it hurt. Make it scary. Make her cry. Make her… Make her… miserable! I don't care what you do. Just make her pay."

Before I know it, I hear commotion over at the shore. I see Isa's dad hurrying toward me, swiftly swimming his way over.

Oh shit. He thinks I came all the way out here by myself. He probably thinks I took the boat, too. I try to climb into the boat and fail. *Oh shit, oh shit.*

When he makes it to me, he gets his shoulder underneath me so I can prop myself in and then he starts swimming while pulling the boat back.

"Oh, my God! Maiana, are you okay?" Isa's mom hugs me, holds me at arm's length, inspecting me, and then hugs me again.

When she releases me, she scolds, "What were you thinking?"

"I—I was playing around. I'm sorry. I, uh, didn't realize how far I went."

"You could have hurt yourself! You could have drowned! You could have been swept out into the ocean! Nen, I *know* you know better than that. Why would you ever do that?" I can tell she is trying to sound non-threatening, but I'm scared about what my parents would do or say. Isa's dad is trying to get a hold of my parents on his cellular phone.

Isa's mom is still going on and on about knowing better, learning lessons and safety, that suddenly I blurted, "I didn't *want* to be out there! I didn't do it!" I regret it instantly. Because what I am about to admit next will sound just as kaduku.

"Oh Lord, did somebody make you?" She turns to the remaining beach goers. "Who did it? Point to them and I'll take care of it."

Wow. I basically turn into putty in her protective nature and the truth spills out of me. "It was a duende."

Isa doesn't hide her surprise in either my honesty or my blatant lie.

Isa's dad finally gets a hold of them. "Håfa adai! It's Isa's dad. I just wanted to let you know there was a little incident—" he goes on, as Isa's mom's eyes are glued to mine, trying to figure out if she believes me or not.

"Okay. Come on, girls." She walks us back to our tent and sits us down. "So, I know your parents are non-believers of the legends, but I must warn you about the duendes."

Holy shit. She actually believes me.

"They... How do I put this... They want friends, and they seem to want to be *your* friend. Sounds nice, right? Maybe you've heard some one-encounter stories, but assuming that this duende or these duendes have been seeing you on a regular basis, that is trouble. That is dangerous. It's a sign that they've latched on to you and they will eventually try to lure you into the deep of the jungle where they live."

I shudder at the memory of last night. I went in on my own. But then he brought me to that hut.

Isa and I share a moment of fear. I can't believe what I'm hearing. She's worried for me but I'm not sure that I've made up my mind yet. I feel like I've got this under control. I would know if I were being lured into a jungle, but even then, I would just not go.

"There are kids who have gone missing all throughout our history—how is it that you can get lost and never found on an island not even forty miles long? You would think they'd be found eventually, lest the ocean pull them, but it is said that where they live in the jungle, they're not actually *here* on this island. So if you get lured, you'll be gone."

Gone? The heck does that mean, *gone?*

Isa breaks the silence. "I've never ever heard of that before. You've never told me that part."

"That is what we older CHamorus were taught and believed. Well, obviously it's stuck with some and not others. Growing up with these stories, it makes sense, and best not to take your chances. Better safe than sorry."

Isa asks what I was thinking, "What do you mean gone? Where do they go?"

"There is a long lost legend that nobody tells anymore, but in my great grandparents' time, they grew up hearing stories of an island that looks reachable. Many have tried to boat there, fly there, but this island does not exist."

"Huh? But Mom, how is that possible? That doesn't make any sense."

"Well, people have concluded that it exists, just not in a physical form. That's how people had begun to explain it because not everyone can see it. And those who have seen it are spiritual people. And not a single non-believer has ever claimed to have seen it. Many believe it to be a sort of spirit island. And that's where I and others believe these lost children who are taken by the duendes must be. Because where else if not here on this island?"

"How come you've never told me this before?"

"Nen, like I said, it's a forgotten legend." She turns to address me. "You need to stay far away from the duendes. Tell it you don't want to be friends and it will leave you alone. Just keep telling it until it's finally gone."

I nod my head in agreement. And I do agree. I just... need him to do this one thing first.

13

—·—

▶❙❙

"One month.

"That's how long we had to enjoy the absence of her taunts before her ultimate demise. And ours as well, I suppose. I hoped it would knock her down a few pegs, and I wanted her to stop picking on everyone. I wanted her to know fear—the fear she made us all feel. If she didn't know fear, then she didn't know helplessness. And if she didn't understand feeling helpless, then how would she understand that what she was doing was wrong? I thought it would make her stop," Nathan doesn't take his eyes off me, laser-focused on my words.

"Of course, at nine years old," I continue, "I didn't have fully-developed critical thinking skills, but it still makes sense looking back on it now. I mean, was it so bad that I wanted to show her that? Nobody was teaching this freaking girl how to behave or how to play nice with other kids. I just wanted to do something. Anything. And so... I told Atte... to make it so that she feels alone.

"Isa, clearly the rational one in our duo, didn't like me having a duende friend anymore. She'd told me that she'd had some nightmares and that maybe she was having them to warn me about the creature. Like, it was a bad omen. She told me she had a bad feeling, and that I should listen to her mother and to stop hanging out with it. I obviously didn't listen to her. Not right away, at least. I felt like I needed to do this for us. I needed to finish Nevaeh.

"I didn't know how it was gonna go down and I didn't want to know. But the change was not what I was expecting. Like, at all. This was not one month of becoming better. It was one month of her decline."

Nathan looks down at his notes and requests, "Walk us through what that time was like."

"I remember the first week where she wasn't a bother to me and Isa. It was nice not to have a single mean look in our direction. It was nice not crying in the bathroom. It was nice to feel like she was minding her own business for once.

"Week two, Atte was nowhere to be found, but the Tweedles, all of them, were no longer giving us any unwanted attention. We were all kids just being kids interacting like kids, not that Nevaeh's spoke any words to us, but Kimmy and Junie had. We had a talent show coming up and Napu joined Isa and me in our act. Junie and Kimmy would watch us practice our little musical song and we'd watch them do a choreography to a Britney Spears song. Sure, we'd still get an occasional death glare by Nevaeh, but there weren't any more plumerias. No more pointing and laughing at me.

"Week three, something was off. She'd get sent to the principal's office for falling asleep in class. She'd get sent to see the nurse for the dark circles around her eyes. But that wasn't my problem. Isa, Napu, and I were too busy getting hyped and ready for the talent show. Isa reminded me that I wanted to be a writer, so I wrote the song we performed. Without the worry of what Nevaeh may or may not do to me, I felt like my brain could breathe again.

"The fourth week..." I take a deep breath, "this was the last full week anyone would ever see her again. Had anyone just gave enough of a damn they would have seen the signs of *something*.

"Meanwhile, I was making fun memories with my best friend without any wish to hide ourselves. We were carefree kids at last, on a mission to win at least third place for the show. I remember I could feel my bitterness melting away.

"I wondered if Atte was finished. I wondered if he would ever come back. It was all very strange. And it all came and went too fast to ask questions or enjoy it or hate it. Knowing we share a world with magical creatures just beyond human reach was totally worth having to deal with life's hardships. At the time, I thought he was free of me and I of him. Nevaeh was free of bullying and Isa was a freer spirit. Nevaeh was going to see that she couldn't walk this world having chased everyone away. I felt that she would be happy someday because of me. And when she was finally ready for a helping hand, I'd hoped that she'd get it.

"And then the night of the talent show happened."

14

MAIANA/NOW-GHOST

"So, how did it go? Did you get grounded?"

"Take a guess. I scared your parents and I wasn't playing safe. Yeah, I'm grounded. They gave me extra chores and I'm not allowed to slack on them."

"Dang. I'm sorry. Man, things have been really weird lately, haven't they?"

"Pfft, tell me about it!"

"Shhh!" the librarian shushes, lost somewhere in the sea of bookshelves.

She twirls the pencil in her hand nervously. "Change is coming." The pencil stops twirling as her mind goes somewhere else.

I don't like the thought of change. "Hey, when we're in middle school next year, are you still gonna be friends with me?" I ask, breaking her out of her odd spell.

Isa doesn't hide her shock. "Maiana! Of course! Why would you ask me that?"

I shrug. "You're the reason I'm not alone in this school. You're gonna meet other cool kids. I'm worried you're gonna leave me behind."

"Maiana, stop. You're talking crazy."

"I'm just scared that we're not going to stay friends forever. I've got this... bad feeling. I don't know."

"Good morning, ladies!" says the librarian who shushed us. This is for you." She places a couple of papers on the table. "Hope you girls can join in on the fun!" She proceeds to pass out the papers to the other tables.

I take my copy, and Isa reads hers. "A talent show?"

It's a permission form. Isa's smile is undeniable. She wants to join, and she wants me to do this with her. I roll my eyes.

"Alright. So, what are we going to perform?"

Her squealing gives me butterflies, already making me nervous at the thought of being on stage with a room full of people watching us.

"Shhh!"

We giggle some more, but quietly this time.

The bell rings, signaling us to get to class. We discuss what talents we have the whole way, trying to figure out what our performance could be. We both like to sing and dance, so we're thinking of some sort of musical performance.

Napu comes over to ask what we look so excited for. We give him a flier and overload him with all our musical ideas, outfit ideas, and practice days.

"I know how to play the ukulele if you guys need an instrument!"

Isa is so excited that someone else wants to join our performance. They start speaking more to each other than with me. I don't mind. I think they *like* like each other. It's so nice to see Isa enjoying herself, not worried about the now-ghost in our lives. *We don't see her, we can't hear her.* That was our pact. She will not ruin this one life we have.

My gaze wanders aimlessly and Nevaeh and I lock eyes. I want to scream at her. *You are not in my life! You merely exist in it!*

I'm not perfect. I know this. But in trying to cope with my own discomforts in life, I'm slowly learning things about myself.

I'm not quick to anger, I just haven't mastered self-control yet. I'm not sensitive, it's just that everything feels big when you're little. I'm not laughing at you, I just haven't developed enough to fathom how serious some things are. I'm not a scaredy-cat when anyone would be afraid of the unknown. I'm not confused, I just haven't learned that yet. And I don't hate you, I'm just... hungry.

Nevaeh looks like she's in a trance. I can't do this stare down any longer, so I push the two along, keeping us moving to our classes, but mostly just to get out of her view. Out of sight, out of mind. For both our sakes, really. Isa and I made a deal that we would act as if she is invisible. She doesn't exist unless she has to. I will stop apologizing to her for no reason and she will stop using the furthest exit just to avoid her. We will not be scared of her any longer.

But she will be scared of Atte.

15

NEVAEH/CAGED-GIRL

"I already told you! I don't know where it is!"

"What, did you sell it or something? You sold it, didn't you?"

"Why would I give it to you as a gift and then sell it behind your back? That doesn't make any sense."

"I don't know, you tell me! God, Nevaeh, I told the guys I was going to bring it next time we go out on the water and now I'm gonna look like an idiot!"

"Dad, I swear to you, you were the last one with the binoculars! Why would I take it?"

"Stop back-talking me!"

I start to sob, trying to keep it to myself, but he can clearly see it. Me showing any weak emotions is Dad's pet peeve.

"Ugh, come on. You don't need to be doing that. I didn't even spank you," he says, sounding remorseful, but I know damn well he's not.

"Sorry. I just really don't know where it is. And I'm not back-talking you. I have never touched it since I found it and gave it to you. I swear to God."

I can tell he wants to keep taking his frustration out on me even though he knows that I'm telling the truth. I can tell he feels stupid for misplacing it himself. Not my fault. We both know it.

Sometimes I force myself to cry because when I do, he becomes a little softer. Sometimes. But at the same time, he hates it when I'm soft. Is it because he wants to raise a tough girl who can handle herself? Or does he want me tough enough to take his verbal hits whenever he needs a punching bag? I don't know. I want to be tough for myself, definitely, but sometimes it's easier to just take it and move on.

"Fine. Whatever. Don't forget to feed the roosters after school." We exit the house at the same time. He gets in the truck and I walk to the bus stop. We don't say goodbye, we don't say I love you. He only does that when he's in a good mood. And he's only in a good mood when he wins cockfighting money. Yeah. I picked up on that pattern a long time ago.

When I get to school, I head to first period, math class, and try to do my homework before the bell rings. I have three questions left when the bell rings and Ms. Flores starts her lesson.

"Nevaeh, can you please come up and solve this problem?" I hate when Ms. Flores calls me up to the board. She knows damn well I will not solve it. And it's the same thing almost every time, that if I don't go up, Miss Smarty Pants Maiana will get called on to solve it. I hate her. She's such a fucking show off. Well, if I had parents who would help me with my studies, maybe I would love to answer the board questions, too.

School was created to make an embarrassment out of me. I'm sure of it. So I say fuck it. If Dad doesn't care about it, then neither do I.

Now, what Dad does care about are his damn roosters. I've come to sort of care about them too, because a lot of the time it's just me and the roosters at home, though I try not to feel any attachment. I feed them almost everyday after school, watch TV, try to do my homework—when I can focus long enough to do it, that is. I don't like feeding the roosters. I feel so bad for them. They're stuck in their cages day and night. I hate that there's nothing I can do about it. I've always wondered if when they see me, they hate me for not freeing them. I used to apologize to each one as I poured food for them but then I stopped because it seemed meaningless. I even try to avoid looking at them anymore.

I am almost done with my after school chore of feeding them when I hear someone's voice. It's faint. I put the chicken food down and go into the house, thinking maybe Dad has come home early.

"Dad?" He's not in his bedroom. And his truck isn't even outside.

Weird.

I go back out to finish my awful chore. I'd rather wash dishes. I'd rather do laundry. I'd rather clean the toilet. Anything else but feed these birds. On top of that, the sun is brutal today. Our broken aircon is icing on the cake. And the foul smell of bird shit is only adding to my irritation. All the windows are open and the two fans are oscillating on full blast, so at least there's that. I pour food for the last cage and begin to head back inside when I hear crying. I look up in the cage on instinct... and there's a girl in there.

"Ahhh!" I fall backwards. There is a girl in the cage! She is hunched over with long dark brown hair covering her face. I can't see it at all. My breathing quickens. What the hell is a girl doing in Dad's rooster cage? She grumbles something that I can't make out.

"What?" I ask softly, more to myself than to her. I move my head just a tiny bit closer to try to hear her better. Holy shit. She's making rooster sounds—the little bawks that they do, the ones that guilt me. Sometimes I imagine they are begs for help. Is that what this girl is doing?

"What are you doing in there? You shouldn't be playing around here. How—How did you even get here?"

I put my hands over the cage to lift it up as soon as my fingers slip between the metal slits, the girl lifts her head at me suddenly and I see her face. I see *my* face. *That's my face! Why does she have my fucking face?*

Except the eyes are too big. Those are not my eyes. And the skin is rough. That's not my skin. But... it looks just like me.

It pops the cage away and lunges at me.

I scream and fall backward.

I scream.

And scream.

And scream until I realize I need more air in my lungs to keep on screaming.

I scramble away from it as quickly as I can. My eyes are watering and I use the back of my hand to wipe my vision clear. I don't want to lose track of it for a single second. And yet, the two seconds it took to wipe my eyes were two seconds too long because… she was gone. I stare into the cage and there is only a rooster.

My heart is pounding at an alarming pace. I can't control my breathing and I feel like I'm going to pass out. I'm on the ground in the dirt. My tailbone hurts. There's just a rooster in there. A freaking rooster. I look around as if there is anyone around to see if they saw that, too. Of course nobody did. There's nobody but me. Always just me.

When Dad finally pulls up I beg him to let me go bird fighting with him tonight. He likes it when I ask to go. And I go ahead and let him think that it's because I'm interested in it even though I always ditch him at the fighting pit.

I sit at the swing set only a few feet away, from the fighting pit, right at the edge of the dark. I can't stop staring into it. I feel like at any moment there's going to be the me that's not me running toward me. I'm not going to look away. That's probably when it'll strike.

I feel like maybe I'm staring too long… because I think… my mind is beginning to imagine that something really is there, just hiding. Watching me. My mind is forming an outline of something that isn't there. *Nothing is there. Nothing is there. There is nothing there.*

I squint. I stare. So fixated on this outline from my imagination.

I feel a hand on my shoulder and I scream.

"Whoa! Hey! It's just me. Sorry." He looks out toward the darkness where I was so focused the last I-don't-know-how-many-minutes. "What are you looking at?"

I take a slow breath in and let it out just as slowly. "Nothing," I laugh. "Where were you? You guys are late."

"Eh, it's nothing. My dad got out of work a bit later." He holds out an opened bag of chips and I refuse. "Uh... are you sure you're okay? Your hands are shaking."

"Yeah, well you scared me."

"Since when do you get scared?"

Since today. Since realizing that maybe whatever was following me after Maiana's house may have followed me home and followed me here.

My eyes glance back to where I was so focused before. I must still be imagining things because the thing my eyes were forming, it's still there. Waving.

16

NEVAEH/DIE

I've not been sleeping well. When I close my eyes all I see is her—the girl who apparently was never actually there. I now have this constant uncomfortable sense that I'm not alone in my house; that I'm being watched walking home and sometimes I even feel it at school. Whenever I see a reflection of myself, I think I'm seeing cage-girl. I'm getting very tired. I can't stay home if I'm not sick, though. Dad won't allow it. I tried. He thinks he's doing right by me by forcing me to school even though I can barely even think. I've told him I'm scared at night. He told me there's nothing to be scared of. I told him there are things lurking in the dark. He said I sound crazy.

"Bottom line, I can't sleep. I'm scared. Can you just stay home tonight?"

"How about I stay home tomorrow night, sweetie? I can't miss poker."

"Can I go with you, then? I won't bother you, I promise!"

"Tsk, I will stay home with you tomorrow, okay? I promise. I'm just down the road, anyway."

Yeah. A long road.

"You can call me if anything happens."

And endure the wrath of a drunken you? No, thanks. I won't make that mistake again.

Fine. I'll just be on my own. I'll just call someone and beg them to stay on the phone with me. That should be fine.

Dad says bye to me this time. I know he feels bad and he just can't help it. He's explained to me many times before that he and Mom had me at a young age and he's trying to catch up on doing things with his friends. I get it. I'm still scared, but I get it. I think.

I make myself an ichiban because that's all we really have. I put the TV on something fun and call up Junie as I eat. Her mother answers and says she can talk but not for too long.

"Hello?"

"Hey, my dad left me alone again. What are you doing?"

"My mom is about to show me how to make chicken keleguen. That's what we're going to have for dinner."

Mmm. That sounds a helluva lot better than this—the thing I eat everyday. "Oh, cool. My dad got me McDonald's. Are you allowed to stay on the phone with me while you guys cook?"

"Hold on, let me ask."

I take three bites of my non-McDonald's dinner before she answers.

"Uh... Sorry. She said I can't."

"Well, can I come over? Or spend the night? I'm by myself and I'm scared to be alone."

She laughs. The bitch is actually laughing. "You? Feeling scared? Wow, I didn't know you could feel anything."

Without responding I hang up. I call Kimmy.

"Nevaeh?"

"Yeah. Are you allowed to stay on the phone with me?"

"Uh…"

Her hesitation is valid. I know I've been mean. I know that I *am* mean.

"Okay. For what, though?"

I roll my eyes. It's so humiliating having to say that I'm scared over and over again. "My dad's not home and it's dark."

"Okaaay," she says again as if asking *And?*

I sigh. "Can I come over?"

"I don't think you can come over right now."

I hang up the phone. She's useless, too. What do I have friends for if they're not going to be of any use to me?

After I finish my ichiban I wash the dishes. I grab my blanket from my bedroom and lay on the couch with the TV (and every light in the house) on. I begin to relax. I start to get sleepy. Maybe I'll be okay for tonight.

Riiing. Riiing. Riiing.

My eyes shoot open. I never realized how loud this stupid phone is. I hop up off the couch hoping it's Junie or Kimmy calling to stay on the phone with me or that I could come over after all. Or maybe it's Dad calling to check up on me.

"Hello?"

"Hello?" someone echoed in *my* voice.

My fingers lose grip on the phone and it crashes onto the floor. Now the voice is speaking very loudly. I can hear what it's saying without the receiver remotely close to my ear.

"Can I come over?" it replays my request from earlier. "Can I come over? Please? I'm scared! I'm a big baby! I need my daddy! Help me! I'm gonna die! Die! DIE! DIIIE!"

"Stop it! Stop it!" I jump back on the couch and curl up, covering my ears and closing my eyes, wishing for my mom.

17

—— ◆ ——

NEVAEH/MOM

Why isn't anybody helping me? Why is my teacher and the school staff and my friends allowing me to come to school this exhausted? A stupid phone call to my dad to inform him that I'm always sleeping in class? Really? Does nobody know my dad? You think he had a talk with me? No. I get in trouble, yes, but he's not even truly concerned about why I'm so tired in the first place. Has he asked me why? Yes, but was he actually interested in the answer? No. That's why I'm still going to school and sleeping in class.

What he has noticed, though, is that I'm barely eating. If your child is skinny, then you must not be a good parent. I guess I'm even skinnier these days. Dad has never cared about what anyone's thought of my slim body. He'd tell everyone that I get it from Mom. But he's been cooking these last few days. It's weird. Nice, but weird. He made red rice and barbecued short ribs, pancit the night after, titiyas for breakfast one morning that lasted two days. I can't remember the last time he made any sort of fiesta food just for us. And he may still be sending me to school, but at least he lets me sleep until dinner's done. He never checks if I have homework either.

While he's in the kitchen blasting a Ben Lam Lam CD I'm sitting under the stars.

"Out of the blue... I'm missing you... Mom," I say, hoping the words will reach her in heaven.

The wind blows gently, as if she is trying to tell me she misses me, too.

"The first thing I remember you for is your hugs. The way they were always so snug and warm. And feeling your heartbeat against my face was a comfort I never thought I'd crave. The second thing I remember you for is your coffee. You let me try it once and I spat it out. You laughed and said that black coffee is for women who have got shit to do. The last thing I remember you for is your beautiful face. Sometimes when I look in the mirror I think I see you. But now, I see a monster that haunts me and I don't know why."

Tears start to fall and all I feel is pain in my heart. Pain like no other.

In a voice so soft and beautiful, I hear, "Nevaeh?"

I shoot up. "Mom?" I ask as if it is the most natural thing for me to hear her voice.

"My sweet neni girl, don't cry. Mommy's right here."

I choke up at the sound of her voice. "Mommy?"

There is an unsettling stillness all around me. I don't even hear Dad cooking or his music anymore. I wait, listening for where the next sound, any sound, will come from.

There it is. A rustling from the jungle.

I don't want to go in there. I stare into it. It's not taking in any of the moonlight. "Come on, neni girl," Mom calls. "You can do it."

A hand from the jungle reaches out to me.

Mom has finally come to take me out of this hell.

I take her hand.

The moment I step in I feel a strong pinch on my right arm. I scream in pain for only a moment because the hand keeps tugging. Cautiously, I allow it to pull me through the tall wild grass and unruly groups of trees. It's taking all of my attention to try not to trip or run into anything. I can't see much from shielding my face from bugs and low hanging branches and leaves until we come to an abrupt stop.

When I open my eyes, I can't... I can't believe what I am seeing. A cleared land with lush grass and an old school CHamoru hut built on latte stones. Eventually I realize that I'm no longer holding a hand. And I must be seeing things. This place can't be real.

"Neni girl, Mommy's up here."

I go up the ladder of the hut and I halt when I see her. Now that she's here in front of me I feel very confused. "You're supposed to be dead."

She shakes her head. "Ahi, girl, I'm right here," she says as she waves my words away. "Come. I've been waiting for you." She pats the floor beside her.

I climb the rest of the ladder and sit next to her. She stares at me, smiling. I stare back in awe. She's so beautiful. "What are you doing here, Mom?"

"You're tired."

Suddenly I'm remembering how true that is. My yawn is heavy.

"Nen," she pats her lap, "rest your little head. You've been through so much."

I wonder how she knows this, but it doesn't matter now. It can matter after I've gotten some rest.

"Huuu guaiiiya hao," she starts singing, *"Huuu guaiiiya hao, it means I love you with all my heart, and I hope we'll never part, 'cause you're meant for me, and me for you."*

I joined her. *"Huuu guaiiiya hao, huuu guaiiiya hao."*

Her fingers comb through my hair as she hums and the gusty air that playfully surges through the tall grass is so calming, it sounds like ocean waves. I can feel my exhaustion fading away. My tiredness is transforming into peace, my fear into tenderness.

Time doesn't exist here. I could have been here thirty minutes, it could have been two hours. The best part, I feel like my energy is slowly being replenished without having to actually fall asleep. I don't want to sleep, not while Mom is here with me. It is blissful—until...

"Nevaeh!"

My eyes open.

"Nevaeh!" the voice says angrier.

I sit up. "Dad?" I climb down the ladder.

He sees me and is shouting at me. "I've been looking for you everywhere! Why are you even out here?" Before I can answer he grabs my hand and starts dragging me back home. When it finally hits me that I'm heading out of the jungle I start to panic. "I say I want to stay a bit longer!" I beg. I pull and pull to go back but there is no budging.

"Absolutely not, Nevaeh."

"Please! Please, Dad! I want to go back! Mom's there!"

He stops abruptly. Freezes in place. "That's not funny." We start moving again but slower.

"Mom is back there! She was combing my hair!"

He doesn't react.

I get loose for a second and turn to run, but when I get back to the spot, it's not the same place that I was in just moments ago. It's not the same place I was led to and pulled out of. That place is no longer here. What *is* here are yellow eyes—many of them—watching me.

I scream my lungs out and run past Dad.

Where did Mom go?

I need her.

I *need* her!

18

NEVAEH/MAIANA'S MONSTER

I hate seeing Napu talking with those losers. Maiana is so shy it's annoying and Isa... well, I gave her what she deserved a couple weeks ago. Though, it doesn't seem to have scared her away from talking with Napu. Doesn't seem like she's bothered by it at all, actually. I hate her.

The bruise on my arm is the size of my hand and hurts like hell. I don't recall injuring myself but I do remember the pain I felt when I entered the jungle. Dad says it must have been a taotamo'na since I didn't ask for permission, but I don't care. I'd do it again to see Mom. Junie and Kimmy laughed when I told them what happened and I laughed with them. In such a short amount of time I've forgotten how to be me. I don't know what I'm doing anymore. I'm just... tired.

They're talking my ear off about the talent show tomorrow. All week they'd shown me the dance so that I could do it with them at least once but honestly, I don't even see what they're doing. I'm looking at them but I'm somewhere else. They're dancing and yet all I see is Mom through my heavy eyelids. I want to remember her that way. Remember the affection of a mother to a daughter.

"Nevaeh, how'd we do this time?" Kimmy asks.

When I get out of my thoughts, I see that creature of mimicry instead of Kimmy. Shocked to see the me that was in the cage, I fall backward off the bench. I can hear the girls' laughter but my eyes are darting everywhere for the copycat. "What the hell are you? What do you want from me?"

The girls stop laughing. Kimmy frowns at the odd attention directed at her.

"You're the devil. You're the freaking *devil.* Leave me alone!"

I'm sure some of my peers think I'm just messing around, I'm sure some are thinking I am genuinely losing my mind, and the rest ignore my behavior.

Later that night, Dad cooks something for dinner but doesn't stay. As I'm watching TV, the me that's not me is on the other end of the couch watching me watch TV. All I can do is pretend it's not there. I can no longer tell what's real or not anymore. I mean, this can't be real, right? It just can't. These last few weeks have to be just one long nightmare. I need to wake up.

And if I am awake, I need to sleep. Only Mom can give me that. I put a plastic chair by the jungle where I had been pulled in the other night, and I sit and wait to be invited in again. It had to have been Mom. I'll wait all night.

"Huuu guaiiiya hao," I sing, as if it's a signal that would bring her to me. *"Hu guaiya hao means I love you with all my heart, I hope we'll never part, 'cause you're meant for me, and me for you."*

When she never comes, I head inside.

"I thought—How did you—Weren't you just in your room?"

"Um, no. I've been outside." Dad's pale face keeps looking toward my room. "Are you okay?" He's not okay. Whatever he had witnessed tells me I'm not going in there.

···········

Dad asked Napu's parents if they could take me with them to the talent show. My head is hurting. My stomach is aching. My eyelids want to seal shut forever but I force them to stay open. I have to go to the talent show. Do I actually want to go watch the stupid lack of talent my peers have? No. But I need rest and there is no rest at home. There will be tons of people at this show. I should be safe to sleep there.

"You're missing out."

"I think I'll survive."

"It's fun!"

"It's dumb."

"It's not too late to join Junie and Kimmy. Or you can join my group."

"And play nice with Isa and Maiana? No, thanks."

"You know, you should really rethink the way you treat my friends. If you can't get along with them—"

" —then one of them is gonna end up crying on the ground again," I laugh.

"If you can't get along with them, then I can't hang out with you anymore."

I don't like the sound of that. In fact, I hate the sound of that.

It makes me want to hate Napu. It sounds like he's made his choice. He's right, though. I can't keep doing what I'm doing. I mean, look at me, I'm a mess!

I sit with Napu's parents, somewhere not that close to the stage. I try to wait for the lights to dim before allowing myself to get comfortable enough to close my eyes. My eyelids are getting heavier and heavier by the minute. My surroundings become blurry. My eyeballs are rolling to the back of my head. Finally, I feel the sweet relief of my eyelids give in. I drift, fast. No scary me, no stupid friends, no failing grades. No Dad.

Just Mom. She's tucking me into bed. I don't remember getting ready for bed but I guess I must have. She's telling me goodnight, smiling at me, kissing my forehead.

"I'm so happy you're here," I choke.

"Me too, nen," she says softly. "Do you want me to tell you a story to help you fall asleep?"

Wow. I haven't been told a story in forever. Probably never. Or maybe I was too young to remember her stories before she died. "Please."

I close my eyes and she strokes my hair back. "Once upon a time, there was an island far, far away from here. It is invisible to any ordinary person's eyes. Only special people can see it. Only the people who the island wants to take can see it. If you have a purpose there, then it finds a way to lure you out to the horizon."

This feels right. This is love. This is all a parent has to do. I hope she will tell Dad that he's been doing it wrong and then he will fix himself and I will become a better person. We will both become better for each other and then he'll remember that he loves me and remember how to love me.

"You, Nevaeh, are one of the special ones. You have a... a glow about you. You have a red aura. The island can feel your anger and it sees who you really are. You're bad, Nev."

My eyes shoot open.

"The island wants you. It wants to save this island from people like you. Horizon Island will save you from yourself, nen."

"Mommy... you're scaring me."

She places a hand on my tummy, rubbing it, trying to soothe me. Then she stood up, hand still rubbing me, her arm outstretching too long. And now that I'm staring at her face, her eyes are a bit too big. This is not Mom.

In my voice she says, "Let's go to Horizon Island. Wake up. We'll go together." The long arm bounces me in the bed, telling me to wake up.

I wake. I see Mom sitting beside me, dancing to the kids on stage. I rub my eyes trying to remember where I am. I would have been happy to see her if I hadn't remembered that she's dead. Then I remembered the dream. I jump out of my seat and scramble through the aisle to run away. When I turned around to see if she's following me, it was no longer her sitting in that chair. It was just some person who came for the show. It doesn't matter, though. I don't feel safe here the same way I don't feel safe during school or at home. I don't know where to run, but I run. I don't even think of where I'm going. I run out through the nearest exit, which brings me to the back of the school, and down the road in the direction of my home. It is a far distance on foot but I don't have any other options. It probably won't even matter. It follows me everywhere.

It's dark and empty along the road. No cars pass by. I'm all alone.

Always alone.

"Who are you?" I ask with the intention of bravery.

Crickets.

"Show yourself, coward."

As I walk down the dark, empty road, something emerges. First it's two floating yellow dots. I've seen those before.

They're coming closer.

And closer.

They're so close now I can reach out and touch it. It's a creature with long, lanky arms. Rough skin. It moves non-threateningly, but I can't be fooled by this monster.

Nothing happens for what feels like a long time. All is quiet. All is still.

"Are you the one that's been—" is all I manage to speak before it zooms right at me and grabs me by the arm. It moves faster than humanly possible and before I know it, I'm on the ground, slowly getting dragged off the road. I groan with pain and the breath is knocked out of my lungs. When I regain enough composure, I see a blur of a person. A real person. My vision clears. "Maiana?" I reach my hand out to her, hoping she will just take my hand knowing I can't get words out.

She addresses the monster. She calls it by a name. *Atte?* She asks this thing what it's doing and why it's taking me. She speaks softly with it. I don't know what it's saying but she can clearly communicate with it and clearly has before—many times before, it seems.

"You... You know this thing? Oh my God, did you plan this? You are a sick fuck! Get me out of here!" I stretch and reach and beg. Her hand is reaching out of mine, just not fast enough. "Hurry up! This is your fault. I know it! Get me out of here! You're a freaking monster and I'm going to tell everyone! You'll regret ever messing with me, you ugly bitch!"

But suddenly, I'm being pulled away once more, this time with such force and speed, I lose sight of Maiana quickly. It's taking me deep into the middle of nowhere in a jungle. The bumpiness of the road burns my skin. The rocks and pebbles. I feel it all. From the ground, all I see is tall grass. The blades of sword grass hurt as they slide across my skin. I scream from pain and in desperation for anybody to hear me. When it finally stops, I am on the verge of passing out.

"Mommy, Mommy," I can barely breathe. I can barely see from the tears and dirt or sand in my eyes. I don't bother to try to get up. I see the monster standing over me. It only stares. "Please," I plead deep within my gut, "Don't hurt me. Don't hur—" My words fade. I can't speak. My entire body begins to quiver.

In my voice it says, "You will stay here now. You will be my friend. You don't have any friends. I can be your friend."

"I w-w-want to go home," I weep.

"Your own father doesn't want you."

I cry harder from how true that has always felt.

"Your mother loved you. Do you want to be with her?"

"She's dead!" I scream.

"I know."

A shock of realization hits me of what the monster means by this. "Please don't k-kill me! Please! I don't want to die!" I can feel everything leaking from my eyes, nose, and mouth.

"Perfect," it smiles. "So I guess that means you're staying."

19

MAIANA/SHOW TIME

They see me. I'm scared. I shouldn't be. I know I shouldn't be. I've been preparing for this. I got this.

"We got this!" Napu says.

Moments ago, I was watching Junie, Kimmy, and someone else do a choreography to Britney Spears' *"Baby One More Time"* and they were actually not bad at all.

Napu grabs me by the shoulders. "Hey, don't be nervous. We're gonna be great."

"I think I'm going to throw up."

Isa hears me. "You can't! Do you see them?" She gestures out to Junie's group. "We need to beat them. I want to shove first place in their faces!"

"But everyone is singing along; everyone loves that song! Nobody will know our song. Oh, this was a bad idea! Why did I ever let you talk me into this?"

Isa smiles at that. "Exactly! I think that will be even better. They're all going to wonder who our song is by and we get to say, 'Oh, this? This is a Maiana Champaco original.' Wouldn't that be cool?"

"I mean, I guess."

"Oh, come on now, get excited!"

"I guess!" I shout with enthusiasm.

"Not what I meant, but okay! Great! Woo!"

"Junie's performance comes to an end and the entire audience is booming with cheers and applause. How the hell are we going to stand a chance against that? The anticipation is building inside me. It feels as though the cheering goes on forever and the announcer has to shush everyone. Ugh. If we lose, I feel like it will give Nevaeh and her friends all the more reason to give us shit. The trio exits the stage wearing smirks and brimming with confidence.

"Now, without further ado, please welcome the musical group—"

Deep breath in. Hold it.

Five... four... three...

" —The Nenis and Napu!"

... two...

Applause.

... one.

Exhale. The applause is excited but not bursting. Napu walks onto the stage first with Isa as I hesitate behind. Napu takes a seat on the stool with his ukulele. Isa takes a standing spot beside him, looking like such a CHamorita with her long wavy hair in her banana leaf printed mestiza dress. I'm wearing the same dress but she totally rocks it. I take it all in as I approach the mic.

The audience is silent and staring. Nevaeh is asleep. Rude. Mom and Dad are in the third row on my right side. They wave at me and I can't bring myself to wave back. Isa's parents are sitting next to them. From my peripheral vision, I see that Isa is waving back. Napu is waiting for me to make an introduction, but I don't want to.

A small, "Uhh," slips out and the mic catches it. That really doesn't help.

I look at Isa and she smiles at me. She says, "It's okay. We can skip the intro if you want."

I turn to Napu and mouth at him to just go ahead and start playing.

The first part of our act is a sweet strumming version of the song that I wrote. It's the part that we can dance to. Isa and I move our hips, our dresses swaying like laundry hanging outside on a breezy day. We swirl our wrists while our arms turn to palm trees in the wind to waves of the ocean. We glide side to side as we twirl with grace.

The final strum of the ukulele marks the end of our dance and brings me standing at the mic, leaving Isa standing alone for a solo dance while I sing.

The applause is light and short when they realize we are not finished. I give Napu a nod letting him know I'm going to start.

> *"You're white soft petals on a green stem,*
>
> *Plumeria, please disagree with them.*
>
> *Mom says that my eyes smile,*
>
> *Although it's been a while.*
>
> *Don't want their words to get to my head."*

No one was dancing. It's not that kind of song. This song was meant for all eyes on Isa. All ears on Napu. And all focus on my lyrics. They're engaged and I'm not minding the spotlight at all.

"Your scent is often kinda scary,
It goes with the legend of White Lady.
But I won't let legend scare me,
And you'll tell me that I'm pretty
Amazing just the way that I am."

Isa has the movement of a tranquil ocean—rotating her wrists and slipping her hands that are following the same movement of her swaying hips that are sashaying the bottom of her dress.

I catch a movement in the audience in the corner of my eye. Nevaeh snaps awake and she glares at the man beside her, like she's afraid of him or something.

"I'm just a kid tryna live her life.
Don't bother me with your hate,
And keep the plumerias out of your lies.
Don't bother them with your lame
Reaction to the world cuz you can't function on your own."

She jumps out of her seat and scrambles out of the aisle and through the exit. Where is she going? What is she worried about? I don't see anybody going after her. I don't get it. What the heck just happened?

"Soft white petals everywhere,
Put a plumeria in my hair."

20

—·—

MAIANA/REACHING. SCREAMING.

The three of us run off stage and hi-five each other. It feels awesome having a whole room of adults listen and watch *us*—children. They were interested, or at least some were, and they were smiling. They were listening. Their heads were bobbing to something *we* made! It was incredible. The attention was... intoxicating.

Even the Tweedle gang is talking about the song. I think our original trumped the world's favorite pop princess tonight. Sorry, Britney.

Isa gives me a big hug. "You did it! You really are gonna be a famous writer one day! Maybe a song writer! They really liked it!"

We are buzzing with adrenaline and high from the positive attention... but I just can't put Nevaeh out of my mind. Sleeping through the show and nearly running out on the rest of the performances is kind of messed up. Of course not as messed up as stealing from a younger kid and beating my friend up but something is off with her. Like, really off.

"I'll be back."

Isa nods her head and peeks between the backstage curtains, watching the next group perform.

I sneak around through the back of the auditorium and exit through the same door Nevaeh had gone through. There's no one out here. Nothing but garbage cans. I walk to the front of the school. Still not seeing her.

Then, I hear her scream.

I run as fast as I can in the direction of the sound. I'm still not sure where to go because the scream came and went too quickly. I slow and wander for a few moments until...

"Maiana?" Nevaeh is on the ground. Her hand is out—*for me?*—to take. My gaze goes from Nevaeh to—

"Atte? What are you doing here?"

"The final revenge scare."

I shake my head trying to understand. "You mean you—"

" —Never stopped," Atte says with me.

"No," I whisper in disbelief.

"You... You know this thing?" Nevaeh asks, horrified.

Huh? I'm so confused. Can Nevaeh see Atte? What are they doing together? What is she doing on the ground? What was that scream about? As questions swirl in my head I subconsciously reach out to help her up. "What are you doing on the—"

Before I can finish my question, she starts yelling at me. Threatening me and cursing at me. And calling me bad names. I really am sick of this. Will it never end?

She's supposed to be a ghost to me. *You're not in my life. You just exist in the world.*

And maybe you shouldn't.

Suddenly, it clicks. That's what Atte wants. He wants to take Nevaeh.

I keep my hand just slightly out of reach while I stare into her crying, angry eyes and feel nothing. I only wanted to live happily. Only wanted harmony. Only wanted to feel comfortable in my own skin and in my own little world. If I'm to survive this life that proves to be unfair time and time again I need control. My fingers are a mere inch away from hers. I hold the power this time. I would have saved her had she only been kinder in this very moment.

"You know, kindness would have been the hero in this story... but you chose hate. You choose it every chance you're given. And you... you've infected me with it. And that's too bad. For you."

I don't know if she caught that last part. She was too busy being dragged away.

I turn around, ready to walk away from Nevaeh and never having to think of her again.

GASP.

"Isa!"

Her jaw is practically on the ground, eyes glistening in the faint streetlight. She can't shift her focus away from the jungle. She won't look at me. I can see her mind racing trying to make sense of what she'd just seen. How do I explain this to her? Or rather, how do I convince her to ignore this?

"Isa," I say a little more firmly, putting myself right in her view, "look at me." She resists. "Isa!"

Finally, she blinks.

"Nothing... happened."

"B-But I saw—"

"Isa. Nothing. Happened."

Her brows draw first into confusion then empathy. I watch as her brain pieces the scene together, coming to the conclusion that I am saying this for the reason she thinks I am.

I can almost hear the questions. "I came out here for some air and I thought I heard, I don't know, an animal. It was just a few stray dogs in a fight and they ran off. That's what you saw." I look her dead in the eyes. "They ran off."

Her breathing gets louder and quicker. I step back. "Are you okay?" She retches right in between us. A little bit splashes on both our shoes. "Oh! Here," I hold her hair as she retches some more.

She coughs and spits out the yuckiness. "Sorry. I... got... dizzy."

I take her face in my hands. "It's okay. Listen... it's important we don't tell anyone about this. They might not even believe us and think we, you know, did something."

She is still dazed. I can't tell if she's on my side or not. "I–I saw—"

" —nothing."

"But that *thing*—"

" —is not real."

"But the things that happened to you—"

" —were just stories."

She grabs at her hair, head turning in every direction to see if anyone is out there, too. She sighs frustratedly and starts to cry uncontrollably.

I squeeze her tight in my arms. She wasn't meant to see this. *I* wasn't meant to see this! This wasn't supposed to happen! Why did Atte have to do this? Why? I hate you, Atte! I fucking hate you! I don't want to be your friend anymore!

21

▶‖

“Nobody could have guessed that the talent show would be the last time many of us would ever see her. She was deemed missing over the weekend. Napu's parents had told Nevaeh's dad that she had walked out in the middle of the show and when she never went back in, they assumed she got bored and walked home. Napu said she didn't want to be there in the first place. I guess she didn't want to be at home without her father or something. Her father couldn't seem to recall if she had come home that weekend or not. Apparently, he didn't know what to tell the police and they found that to be very suspicious. They didn't think he or Napu's parents had directly done anything to her but my parents said there was definite child neglect.

"It had been some time since she had gone missing and classmates were slowly forgetting about her. Not Isa and I, though. Every single day that we didn't feel that familiar fear or anxiety from being around her was a reminder that we were the last people to have seen her and only we knew the truth. It made us sick to our stomachs.

"Poor Isa tried very hard to put it out of her mind but I could see that she couldn't. Her brain would not go idle. If something wasn't occupying her mind, she'd zone out and relive the mess I made. The mess I got her into. It haunted her. And that haunted me. I'd tried to tell myself and her that time would erase it all. Yet, the more time passed, the less I'd heard from her. After a few months she pretty much stopped talking to me, although we would still be together at school. Napu would ask us what was wrong and we obviously would say nothing was wrong. We would jokingly say that we were sick of each other, except she would go too hard on that joke to the point where it would make others uncomfortable. She'd laugh it off, though.

"At the end of fifth grade, she had told me she couldn't be my friend anymore. I said that I understood. I thought that it was sad for a moment, for the both of us but it wasn't. I supposed it was quite freeing for her, considering the last words she'd said to me then was *I hate you.*

"I'd infected her with hate."

22

Maiana/Fast Forward

It's been so long since life has felt normal. I know nobody's life is perfect, but I feel like I have completely missed the normal nuance of a developing child. Puberty was nothing I panicked about. Teenage angst was lost amongst the guilt I have for Isa and Nevaeh. I could have hated my parents for not allowing me to go to a school dance or a baseball game but instead they pushed me to them because I only ever wanted to be home. I was so within my own mind that they couldn't be bothered with failing grades, not keeping up with my chores, or even talking back.

My battles with Mom and Dad didn't seem so big anymore. I recall thinking that little things seemed so big to a small child, that is until something big and real had happened, and then there came a clarity one can only discover through experience. I want to go back to the days where my big problems were feeling like I wasn't being heard. Now, I want nothing more than to keep everything to myself. Ain't that some shit.

This man across the table from me, he seems like he's gone through the normal experiences kids should grow up having. No trauma. No crime. He is carefree, aside from the usual stresses of adulthood, of course. I can see that when he looks into my eyes, he's wondering what's on my mind, because I know I'm not present.

"Sorry, I'm—I haven't been in a—on a date in quite some time." Try never.

"Oh, psh, don't even worry about it," he soothes.

An awkward laugh comes out of me. "I just feel like I'm not doing or saying the right things. I feel... like I should... talk more?"

"Hey, I mean, I feel like I should talk less. So, what *is* going on in that head of yours right now? Work? I mean, you don't have to share, it just seems like you're thinking of something rather important."

"I was just thinking about how I sometimes feel like I missed out on so many formative growing experiences... by... shutting myself away from the world."

"Oh? And why did you do that?"

Oh boy. How do I want to say this? "Um... I don't know. I'm extremely shy?" I smile shyly.

"Oh, well then, it's a wonder how I ever convinced you to go on this date with me," he sips his wine with a smug smirk.

"I don't know. I think once you said seafood dinner I knew I had to go. And it didn't matter who with," I tease.

"Ouch," he laughs. And his laugh makes me laugh. "I know it's not what Guam's seafood might be like, but hey, who could say no to Red Lobster?"

He talks about what it was like having grown up in California and I talk about how much less exciting it was growing up on the island. I told him what tourists like to do there because, hell,

I didn't know what I liked doing there. I never did anything. Not after…

"Maybe someday you could take me there and show this tourist around."

Maybe I could take you to where I ruined lives and you'll want to run fast and far away from me. "Maybe."

The vibration of my phone rumbles on the table. I flash him an apologetic smile. "Hi, Mom.," I answer.

"Nen, how did your date go?"

I glance at my date and he is acting like he is paying attention to everything else in the restaurant but my conversation. I cover the mouthpiece and excuse myself from the table.

"Oh, are you on your date right now?"

I don't speak until I'm outside. "Yes, I am in the middle of my date. What's up?"

"So, remember your friend, Isa? She was your elementary friend."

"Yes, of course I do."

"Well, we bumped into her mom at Cost-U-Less and she was saying how much worse Isa is doing since we last saw them. Which waaasss… I don't know, Maiana. Years."

Ugh. "Mom, why are you telling me this? We haven't spoken since we were little."

"That's why I'm calling, nai! She's, uh… having a hard time. Her mom remembers you and how you girls were such good friends. She is wondering if you could give her a call sometime. Like on the video thing. On the internet."

I sigh. "Now?"

"No, of course not. You're on your date. How is your date going? Where did he take you? What did you order?"

"Mom, I don't know."

"You don't know what you ordered?"

God, this woman used to seem so smart to me. I put a finger on my temple. "No, I don't know if I want to call Isa. It's been so long and, I don't know, it's going to be weird. And I'm sure she doesn't know her mom is going around telling people her business of her... you know... mental state. She probably won't like that, right? If she's... going through something?"

"Ugh, Maiana, I'm just letting you know. You're twenty-four and all the way in Cali. I can't make you do anything. She just thinks that hearing your voice might help her."

More like trigger her.

"Napu used to go over all the time a few years ago but he doesn't anymore and she doesn't know why. She thinks Isa probably told him to stop coming around but who knows. Isa is... I don't know. If you want to know how she's doing I'll text you her number and you can reach her on the WhatsApp application. I told her mom that that's how I am able to reach you. The What'sApp application. I told her to put it on her phone."

"That's great, Mom."

"And I gave them your number. I said Isa can call if she finds herself wanting to reconnect."

I take the phone from my ear for a moment to take a calming breath. I know for damn sure Isa still wouldn't want anything to do with me. I'm pretty sure I did this to her. I watched the beginning of this... whatever she's going through... back in middle school. She'd let people walk all over her even more than I let the Tweedles walk on me. Some of our elementary classmates were protective over her, when the new middle schoolers took advantage of her kindness. Her friends saw it. I used to think it was her way of making up for the secret she was keeping. My secret. Napu tried to be there for her, but as one does when they don't think they are worthy of care, she tried to push him away. I saw that, too. And it sounds like she finally pushed him away for good.

"Okay, Mom."

"*Okay* what? Are you going to call her?"

"*Okay,* I'll think about it. I'm still on my date. I have to go." I hang up without saying goodbye or I love you.

Unfortunately, when I got back inside to the nice, sweet guy who was patiently waiting for me, I was even further gone than I already was.

He doesn't ask me on a second date.

When I make it back to my little rental, exhausted from trying to be remotely cute and entertaining yet utterly failing, I take off my little black dress and slip into some pajamas and make a cup of hot tea. I like having tea when I write.

I'm sitting at my desk and continuing a writing project I've been working all year on. It's a book. I'm trying to write a book. I tried to do the whole song writing thing that Isa envisioned I'd pursue because of the talent show, but every time I tried, I'd think of *that* night. So, I had to write off music completely.

This book, though, wasn't a book at first. It started as a way for me to cope. Eventually, it became something that I didn't want to feel shame about. It became something with a happy ending. It became my "*What if*" world to get lost in. It became an escape from my shame and guilt. I could dive in and pretend like what had happened had never happened. I built a world where I saved Nevaeh. I built a world where *that* is what Isa witnessed and she respected me more for it. A world where Napu and Isa end up together and Nevaeh was happy for them. A world where we grew old together as friends.

I'm close to The End and I know how I want to end it. When we're old and gray is when we manage to find the spirit island that Isa's mom had told us about. We all find it by accident while on a boat. And we just... ride towards it. The ocean carefully guides us to the horizon, to witness this long lost legend for ourselves, together. To the setting sun. Our end.

23

—·—

Maiana/Release Day

"Oh, man! The seats are filling up nicely, Maiana!" She closes the office door and squeezes my arms. "This is it. This is what you've worked so hard for these last two years. Your childhood dream of becoming a writer is blooming right now," Beth scans my face. "Why aren't you more excited? Everything you wanted is coming together."

Oh girl, if only you knew. If only you knew that this book was a complete accident sprung from misery. A desperate attempt at keeping myself alive.

"Come on, girl, get excited! This is a great book!"

"You have to say that. You're my editor. Thank you, by the way, for being here with me for this."

"Of course. And I'm not just your editor; I'm your friend. And I'll try not to take offense to that. But you know I'm here for you. For whatever, not just for writing."

As I peek through the same door, I'm feeling the butterflies I had experienced only once before in my life: the talent show. Seeing the bookstore with filled seats, makes me feel like I am in the auditorium once again. Isa and Napu are trying to hype me up. We're smiling and breathing and hoping we don't forget our parts. Finally taking our place on stage I remember not saying what I was supposed to. I still remember the words I didn't speak.

Good evening, ladies and gentlemen. We are The Nenis and Napu and we are going to perform a dance created by Isa and sing an original song called "Plumeria In My Hair" by me. Music by Napu. We hope you enjoy the show. Thank you.

It was such a simple thing to just say. Why couldn't I say it?

And then I remember how Isa said it was okay for me to skip that speaking part. She loved me then. She made me feel like I could never be alone. And I made it so that she only wanted to be alone.

I try to blink that memory out of my head and continue to scan the crowd. I want to see the faces of the people who are the least bit interested in my book. I gasp when I see a woman who looks like what Nevaeh could have grown to look like had she lived to adulthood. And now I see Nevaeh waking up in her seat and leaving the auditorium. I see myself following after her. My imagination doesn't need to follow the two girls to know what happens outside those doors.

I look away and focus on steadying my breathing. I practice my smile when Beth isn't looking.

When the bookstore manager begins my introduction Beth is holding my hand and squeezing it for reassurance. Is it bad that I'm imagining it's Isa holding my hand instead?

The applause is my cue to step out. Even though the event is small, it feels big. I suppose there will always be small things that feel big no matter how big you get.

The memory of Isa telling me it's okay flashes in my mind and I have to blink her away. She can't help me this time. I can do this. "Hello. Håfa adai. Good evening." I see Mom and Dad in the audience. They stick out like a sore thumb with the money leis they will put on me when this is over. It's embarrassing, but so sweet that they continue that tradition with me, their only child.

"I appreciate you for coming to listen to me talk about my debut novel. It's uh... It's been quite a journey. I've never said this before on socials or anything, but before this became even a thought for a book, it was first a healing process for me." I see the looks on my parents' faces. They seem to wonder what sort of *healing* I may have wanted or needed through the years. Not very surprising. They've got a phone pointing at me, to record this I guess.

"I guess I was just healing from being a kid. I didn't know how to deal with bullies. I didn't know how to cope with drifting away from a best friend. I didn't know how to make friends after her. I didn't know how to be around people. I began not liking being around people. I became scared of the world."

I feel like I'm losing the audience.

Oh, fuck. How embarrassing. I've never even properly introduced the book! "The book is called Duende. The duendes are prankster gnome-like creatures that the people of Guam believe, or I guess nowadays, used to believe, were real. When a young girl befriends one, she gets help from it to get revenge on her bully. But also, the duende seemingly has plans of his own." But before he can take it too far I try to stop him and I save my bully and we all live happily ever after.

Okay, good. Getting somewhere. Now, connect it to them. "Duende is about hope. It's about friendship. It's about wanting to be better. It's not only about knowing right from wrong, but acting right from doing wrong. It gets a little messed up in there, and life *is* messy, but it doesn't have to be messy forever. Writing this story gave me a safe space. It made it so that I get to keep my friend. It made it so that in another world, I'm happy."

Mom and Dad are whispering to each other, still looking concerned. Could this be the night we can get a lot off our chests? Would they try to pry me open? Would they shower me with love and understanding? How much would I be willing to tell them? I should keep it vague. Yeah... because they'll probably have a lot of questions about where my mental health has been all these years, because I'm sure they'd been worried but never had the "right time" to be vulnerable with me. Yeah. I'm sure they'll want to pry this time.

When the event was over, Mom and Dad were the last people that came to talk with me before leaving. They were going to go back to their hotel and they'd see me later for dinner to celebrate. The thing with that though, is they were looking at me as if they were almost seeing me for who I really am. For who I'd been all these years. Someone to pity. Is it weird that I am hoping they will ask me one more time about what happened between Isa and I back then?

If there was ever a time to ask it, it would have been that night. But of course they didn't. They asked nothing.

They're still not listening.

·········

They flew back to Guam the next morning. Needless to say, we had an early night. They had been here all week but last night should have been the night. Maybe this is best. Maybe I don't need to tell them that I had been struggling all these years and why. They wouldn't believe me anyway. Hell, they probably wouldn't believe Isa if she ever came out with the truth. Perhaps the universe is telling me that it's not meant to be. They're not meant to know.

I stare at my book. *Duende.* I flip through it and can't help but wonder if after all these years Isa still keeps books close to her. If so, what is her reading list like? How has her taste matured? Would she read my book?

A number that I'm not familiar with is video calling. A 671 area code. I wonder...

I slide the button to answer.

On the screen appears a very slim and pale brown woman. Hair cut above her shoulders. Her lips are cracked but covered in lipstick as if trying to hide it. I don't know this person.

But I know the eyes.

"Isa!" I say louder than I mean to.

"How could you?" No surprise, she isn't happy to see me.

I stare, not knowing what she's referring to.

"Are you deaf? Say something."

I'm too stunned and scared. "How—How are you doing?"

"I saw the whole thing. Your parents had us on video to watch you talk about your stupid book. How could you write such a story? How could you put that out there?"

"It's not the real thing. And I changed all the names! No one will know who these characters reflect."

"It doesn't matter; I don't want that shit out there!"

"No, it's different. It—It ends happily."

She rolls her eyes and says nothing else.

"I'm sorry. I should have asked. But I know that you wouldn't have wanted to talk with me if I tried to."

Silence.

"I miss you."

"I don't miss you."

"So why are you calling me?"

"My mom wanted me to send you our congratulations. I had no choice. She made me."

"At least she didn't make you leave the house." Shit. Looks like this call is going to be filled with regrets.

"Fuck you, Maiana. You ruined my life. Do you know that?"

I nod vigorously and sorrowfully. I shouldn't have jabbed but I can't stand to see her hate me.

"Do you know what seeing her—" she pauses, I guess to listen if someone might be listening outside her door. She whispers, "Do you know what seeing her Missing pictures was like for me? Do you know that I've had nightmares ever since you met that damn thing? I thought maybe it was just something that I was going through for whatever reason, but I've had a hell of a long time to think about weird shit from back then and I think your fucking duende friend was fucking with me, too. Those dreams were fucking terrifying as a kid! And after Nevaeh went missing," she makes quotations with her fingers, "I would have nightmares of your stupid duende and Nevaeh calling out for your help. And my help! She saw me that night. She did. The last thing she saw was not just you leaving her for dead or whatever the hell happened to her, but saw me also doing nothing. Just letting it happen. And I'm still having those nightmares." A barbaric laugh escapes her as she says, "And because of you, I felt like I needed to spend most of my life trying to do good deeds. Like I needed to please others to make up for knowing what I know."

I don't want to say anything because I can feel that she's finally saying all that she's been wanting to say to me.

She almost yells this time. "Are you hearing me? I have lived most of my life living for others instead of myself! Because of you! Because you wanted me to keep this gross secret. And I did because I loved you. I trusted you! I had to tell myself that there was a reason that was happening. Maiana, *why* did you let that happen? Fucking *why*?"

I don't want to lie to her, so I stay quiet. I had no good reason. I was a petty little nine-year-old. I was young. Hurt. Stupid.

She rolls her eyes yet again. "I have this recurring nightmare—it's almost the same every time—where I'm out in the jungle looking for Nevaeh. I'll hear her screaming and I'm calling out to her, letting her know that I'm trying to find her. I'm walking in the jungle the whole time. It feels like an endless jungle."

I know that jungle.

"And the whole time I'm searching for her, this pair of yellow eyes follows me wherever I go. Doesn't matter which direction I'm facing, it makes sure I can see it. Those are the eyes you used to tell me about."

I scoff. "Well, at least you can bet it's not real."

"The duendes can't follow us into our dreams, can they?"

"Of course not."

Can they?

24

—·—

▶❙❙

"Isa's parents had missed the mark when they thought Isa talking with me was a good idea. A few weeks after our call, I heard the news. Just days later, her letter arrived.

"I killed my best friend. Sorry—*ex*-best friend.

"Had I just let her reach me... had I just reached another inch... had I just taken all her bullying—because that's nothing compared to this. The revenge wasn't worth going through all that she went through. And for her to go through it alone? Fuck, man. It wasn't worth the two of us carrying this guilt. It wouldn't have been worth it even if Isa hadn't witnessed anything. It wasn't worth the both of us not enjoying life, not excelling at anything. It wasn't worth either of us slipping away from the relationships of our parents or other friends or potential romantic partners. I'd always believed that she and Napu would end up together. In fact, I had truly hoped that he would be her savior out of her hell—the one I inflicted on her. I would often pray that she would find a way to blame me and only me and move on with her life. I would walk through a million different hells if it meant I could have carried this alone. It wasn't worth losing her then, and now forever.

"I wish I had said more than just 'I'm sorry' that day. I wish I could have said all of this to her instead of you guys. No offense."

"Oh, don't apologize," Nathan says unbothered.

"I wish I could respond to her letter knowing she'd at least be thinking about either reading it or burning it. Now, all I can do is speak the words and let them float into the air hoping her spirit would catch wind of it. And even then, she could still hate me. I just... never imagined that the opportunity for me to apologize in a zillion different ways would be cut anytime soon."

"At least you got to tell her you were sorry."

"Yeah, I want to tell her that I'm not *just* sorry. I am the most sorry anyone in the world could ever be. I want to tell her that it's all my fault and that I should never have made her feel obligated to keep it a secret. I want to tell her that I should have stepped up on my own and gone to an adult with something to say so they could know where in the jungle to have searched sooner. I want to tell her that I know all of this doesn't matter at all now because lives have already been destroyed. Ended. I want to tell her that I don't deserve forgiveness from her or her parents or Nevaeh's dad or anyone else. I know there's a place in hell for me and I'll graciously accept it. I want to tell her that if anyone deserved to leave this world too soon it should have been me. I wish she was the one still alive for the chance to heal. But I'll happily live to suffer. For her. For Nevaeh. It's what I deserve. Living shall be my hell until death parts me from the living."

25

MAIANA/THE STORIES MUST CONTINUE

I let a year pass before visiting Isa's grave. She's buried in the Merizo cemetery. I don't tell my parents I'm home. I want to keep the visit short and personal. I check into an AirBnB in a village farther from Mom and Dad's house because I don't want anyone to know I'm back. It is someplace close to the University of Guam. The college Isa and I, maybe even Nevaeh, should have graduated from. After dropping my things off and washing up a bit I head straight to the cemetery. The farther south I drive, the more vivid my memories of Atte become. In my head flashes the first time I felt like something was following me home. I was singing a Maiana original.

Lights in the ocean.

Fairies in motion.

Feeling emotion.

Devotion.

To me.

Driving through Ipan I pass the beach where I went camping with Isa. Man, that was another life ago. Atte terrorized me there, too. I suddenly recall how he somehow got me far from the shore. I remember how Isa's mom had told us about the legend of the duendes that she grew up hearing about. She warned me and I should have listened. I should have told Atte to go away then and there. On days that I try to show myself some mercy, I like to imagine what life would have been like had I followed that warning. Perhaps Nevaeh would have matured by high school. Maybe she would have become a victim of bullying herself and experienced how awful it feels. Maybe she would have been a mother to a daughter and discovered how badly she'd want to shield her child from people like herself.

Perhaps Isa would have become an author. Or a librarian. Maybe she really would have ended up with Napu and Nevaeh would have learned to be happy for her childhood friend and former enemy. Maybe they could have become friends because of Napu. Maybe I would have been a godmother to Isa's first child. Maybe they would have named their first daughter after me—her best friend.

Before I know it, I'm driving past Quinene Road.

Bye, Mom and Dad.

It is too dark for me to see the sparkles of the waves that I once imagined to be magical little creatures. I'm done with all that now.

Can you feel my energy, Atte? Don't come looking for me!

I would have stopped by one of these mini marts for a quick spam sushi or an empanada but they were all closed. I'm not hungry, I merely have the urge to procrastinate. Minutes later, I made it to the cemetery. I shine my phone light on each grave until I find hers. It takes more time than I had expected. Looking at all these graves makes me sad. I wonder if Nevaeh has an empty grave somewhere here.

I brought a plumeria lei that I got from the airport and placed it on her grave. I laugh at the irony. "No, Isa, I'm not calling you ugly by giving you plumerias." I let out a heavy breath. "Man, for so long... I hated plumerias. Even through the whole Nevaeh thing, I still hated that she ruined the flower for me. I could have just reclaimed it, right? To make it mean something nicer? That's what I tried to do with our song, but then it soured again." I sigh and sit in front of the stone, placing my phone to my side, flashlight up.

"You know, when we were kids I used to think that you and I were on the same level. The same wavelength. Frequency. Whatever you want to call it. I'm sure this is of no shock to you but I was nowhere close. You had more... more... just more common sense. More compassion. As for me, I've never felt so unaware of my unawareness until... well, I can't say. I feel like I'm still in the dark in my own mind. Like I can only see a few feet of what's ahead at a time rather than the whole of my surroundings."

I want to speak to her so badly. In person. I want to look into her eyes as I say these words even though all I'd see in them is disgust.

"Does that make sense? I don't know. Sometimes I also feel like I just make no sense." I rest my elbows on my knees, defeated. "I'm sorry, Isa. I'm sorry for fucking everything up." I sob. I struggle to get my words out. "I fucking hate myself! You deser-deserved better. You deserved so much more in life. I'm sorry. I'm so sorry." Tears drop steadily as my body trembles. I curl up and hug my legs because I can't hug her. I wail into my lap telling Isa how much I hate myself. Her hate for me wasn't enough. I need more of it. I start hitting my head with my hand. Hitting. Hitting.

What if I walk across the street right now and let the ocean take me? My writing spot is only a little ways back... Let God decide if I should live or die. Let Him decide how I live or die. Would I drown? Would I be shark food? Or would He keep me alive as I starve to death for a slow and torturous death?

As I sit here I hear something come up beside me real quick. I don't bother to look but I know what's there.

"I don't want to see you. I don't want you here. She wouldn't either."

Atte shakes something and it sounds familiar. Without looking, I know it's the box of gonggi I had given him a long time ago. I cry harder.

The duendes are not our friends. I believe they're just evil spirits. Fucking evil. All of them! People need to know. Doesn't matter if they think it's just another fairytale. The stories must continue.

26

▶❙❙

"And now here you are, warning viewers and listeners not to take these kinds of things lightly. Things such as legends, folklore, superstitions. But also, come on, people, take care of your kids. See them. Hear them. Teach them. Love them. Do you want to promote your book as well?" Nathan looks at me expectantly. "Tell us more about it."

"No. I don't want to do that."

"Oh, uh, okay. In that case, thank you to my very interesting guest today, Maiana Champaco, from the gorgeous island of, not Guatemala, but Guam. She doesn't want to promote her book but I would like to anyway because it's something very special. I've got my beautiful copy of *Duende*, so go get yours! Are there any last words you want to say to the viewers?"

I look deadpan into the camera.

"Adios."

27

— · —

ADIOS

They can't follow us into our dreams, can they? This question has bothered me for years, since Isa was buried. I have been haunted by the same dreams she'd had about Nevaeh. It always starts with me walking into the jungle from the steep road of my childhood home. Upon entering, I'd get that same sensation I got when I was a little girl, when I went in to find Atte. But in the dreams I'm all grown up. A foot goes in and it feels like I'm stepping into something different. I bring my other foot in and the whole place goes quiet. I'll have this strong urge to call out for Nevaeh. I see the yellow eyes that Isa mentioned—they're the same ones I saw when Atte first came into my life. I never pay them any attention. I'd always remind myself that it's all just a dream... but I was interested in where this would go.

It's weird sleeping in this house without either one of the people who cared for and loved me, even if they didn't do it in the way I wished they would have. I mean, who am I to call them out for being imperfect? I'm sorry I ever thought that they weren't doing enough. They did what they could and knew how to. I take a family photo from the counter, the one down the hall where the house phone is—the one where I heard that frightening conversation with my voice that wasn't mine. I'm not frightened anymore. Nothing will ever frighten me again, really. I'd prepared all my life that should anything bad happen to me, it's what I deserve. It's not any different from being back where it all started. Alone. At night. In complete quiet. I set the framed photo beside my childhood bed so I can have them with me when I sleep tonight, already missing them terribly.

I shower, brush my teeth and hair, and throw on a big shirt. I climb into the twin bed and turn on my clock radio. The Quiet Storm is a discontinued station. All that's on are new hit songs. I want the soft, quiet, poetic oldies.

I drift to sleep almost as soon as my head hits the pillow and the dream comes to me instantly. I already know how this whole song and dance goes. I appear, I see the eyes, I call out her name over and over. Even though I'm used to what the truth is, inside and outside of my consciousness, in the dream I have this dread as if I had just just learned that she had gone missing. Even though I already know I am never going to find her. But not tonight. Tonight I want to find her. I must. Surely I can at least conjure up an ending, whatever ending I want, since it's in my head. That's what I'm going to do. I'm going to find her.

"Nevaeh!"

Nothing.

"Nevaeh! I'm here to bring you home!"

Yellow eyes. I gasp at their sudden appearance but ignore it.

"Please, Nevaeh! I have so much to say to you!"

No matter how far I walk, the path keeps going. Doesn't

matter if I try to turn around, I'm just lost in a sea of tall grass and trees.

"I'm not waking up until I find you! You hear that, Atte?" I spin around, "Since you're going to throw me into this God forsaken dream week after week, I'll find her and take her away from you!"

The eyes move in a different way for the first time since I started having Isa's dream. They blink and the creature tilts its head.

The silhouette of the creature finally reveals itself. "I've missed playing with you."

My eyes grow wide. I'd know that voice anywhere. I'd forced myself not to forget it. But Nevaeh would never say something like that. We've never played together. Never had a nice moment together ever.

"It's me, Atte, you kaduku girl. You gave me this name. Don't you remember?"

I sneer. "Stop using her voice. It's disrespectful. And fucking twisted. And yeah, I remember. I remember more than I care to, thanks to you."

"Oh, good."

"Oh, my God. Are you really not capable of understanding what you've done by taking Nevaeh away?"

"I did it because you wanted me to."

"I didn't want you to do *that!* You had already done the thing you were supposed to. Freak her out—that was all you were supposed to do!"

"Yes, you wanted a revenge scare."

"Yes! A scare, not a kidnapping. And you told me you did it;
the rooster, the cage!"

"*Still* doing it."

My breathing picks up. I feel dizzy. "No," I whisper to myself
because I can't get my voice out.

"Yes," he says.

"I sit on the ground to scratch my bearings. "No. The
scare—with the rooster. Something about a rooster."

"It was all of it."

I look at him, scared of asking the obvious question and even
more scared to hear the answer. "What the fuck do you mean 'All
of it'? What else did you do?" I'm panting harder now.

The smirk Atte is giving me is sending chills up and down my
spine, like electricity is coursing through my body. "Let's see...
She saw herself. I kept her company. I let her see her mother again,
who she misses terribly."

"Missed. She missed her terribly," I say defeatedly.

"No, she still misses her."

I get to my feet very quickly. "Wait... She's still alive?"

Atte smirks again. "I've said too much." In a blink of an eye,
I'm back on my steep road and he's disappeared. When I try to
reenter, I wake.

My pillow is soaked with sweat. I get up to wash my face and
dry my neck. It's only four in the morning. I don't want to go
back to sleep. I don't want to see Atte when I close my eyes. Can
the duendes invade our dreams? Of course they can't. This is all
just me taking in Isa's trauma.

I make myself a cup of coffee and turn on the TV for some

noise. This feels like the TV is babysitting me all over again.

"I miss you, Isa. I miss you, Mom and Dad. Nevaeh… I don't know if I miss you but I'm sorry for everything."

Wait. Did I dream of Nevaeh? Did I finally find her? Wait, no. That was Atte using her—

I'm suddenly recalling the dream! It was different! I ditch my coffee and run outside. I've viewed the jungle differently over the years. In middle school, it was scary. In high school I was terrified and hated it. In my twenties, I barely thought about it. By then I had no life after leaving this island. I started new, sure, but just a new, lonely life. I'm in my thirties and now I wonder what's really in the jungles of the island. I used to think myself fortunate to have stumbled upon these strange happenings. It's no blessing. These creatures are curses. And I am ready to submit to my curse, with which I cursed others. They've both paid the price and I guess it's my turn. Not like anyone will miss me anyway.

"Are you happy? This is what my life has become! You win! Come out and claim your prize. Guella yan guello! May I enter your land?" I hesitate. I feel like this is where my story ends. I feel like if I enter… I should… not return. Not without Nevaeh. She's still alive. That's what I believe. I will find her. I will bring her home.

One foot in, the air is changed. Next foot in, I'm enveloped in this different jungle. So, it has not forgotten me after all this time. It almost feels like a warm welcome, but I know better this time.

Look out for your children or the duendes will look out for them for you. Beware. The legend is real.

Hang out with me! Or follow me
for future giveaways.

✿

TikTok: amandasimons.author

Instagram: amandasimons.author